"How Did I End Up With You In My Arms?"

Grant asked her wonderingly.

Jolene stretched luxuriously beneath his hands. "I don't know," she said softly. "Maybe it was just meant to be."

He stared down at her, shaking his head. "This isn't right."

Jolene looked at him as he rose from the bed. "I'm sorry," she said stiffly. "I didn't mean to intrude on your space."

He turned back to face her. "No, it's not that, it's just…" He started to reach for her again, drawn inexorably and relentlessly toward her by something he couldn't explain—and couldn't let happen. How could he tell her that the man she was really meant to be with was his brother?

He pulled her into his arms again. *Just one more kiss,* he thought irrationally. *Just one.*

Dear Reader,

Hello! For the past few months I'm sure you've noticed the new (but probably familiar) name at the bottom of this letter. I was previously the senior editor of the Silhouette Romance line, and now, as senior editor of Silhouette Desire, I'm thrilled to bring you six sensuous, deeply emotional Silhouette Desire novels every month by some of the bestselling—and most beloved—authors in the genre.

January begins with *The Cowboy Steals a Lady*, January's MAN OF THE MONTH title and the latest book in bestselling author Anne McAllister's CODE OF THE WEST series. You should see the look on Shane Nichols's handsome face when he realizes he's stolen the wrong woman...especially when she doesn't mind being stolen or trapped with Mr. January one bit....

Wife for a Night by Carol Grace is a sexy tale of a woman who'd been too young for her handsome groom-to-be years ago, but is all grown up now.... And in Raye Morgan's *The Hand-Picked Bride*, what's a man to do when he craves the lady he'd hand-picked to be his brother's bride?

Plus, we have *Tall, Dark and Temporary* by Susan Connell, the latest in THE GIRLS MOST LIKELY TO... miniseries; *The Love Twin* by ultrasensuous writer Patty Salier; and Judith McWilliams's *The Boss, the Beauty and the Bargain*. All as irresistible as they sound!

I hope you enjoy January's selections, and here's to a very happy New Year (with promises of many more Silhouette Desire novels you won't want to miss)!

Regards,

Melissa Senate

Melissa Senate
Senior Editor

Please address questions and book requests to:
Silhouette Reader Service
U.S.: 3010 Walden Ave., P.O. Box 1325, Buffalo, NY 14269
Canadian: P.O. Box 609, Fort Erie, Ont. L2A 5X3

RAYE
MORGAN
THE HAND-PICKED BRIDE

SILHOUETTE *Desire*

Published by Silhouette Books

America's Publisher of Contemporary Romance

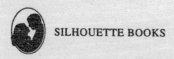

SILHOUETTE BOOKS

RECYCLED PAPER

ISBN 0-373-76119-8

THE HAND-PICKED BRIDE

Printed in U.S.A.

RAYE MORGAN

favors settings in the West, which is where she has spent most of her life. She admits to a penchant for Western heroes, believing that whether he's a rugged outdoorsman or a smooth city sophisticate, he tends to have a streak of wildness that the romantic heroine can't resist taming. She's been married to one of those Western men for twenty years and is busy raising four more in her Southern California home.

One

"Hey, Jolene. What happened to your baby?" the produce man from the neighboring booth called over.

"Kevin?" Jolene Campbell whirled and stared at the empty playpen in disbelief. For half a second, the facts failed to register. It couldn't be. She'd just put him down a minute ago. She'd been talking to a customer and she'd glanced over and he'd been there. He'd been there!

But he was gone now.

One side of the soft foam playpen was smashed down and she knew right away her adventurous eighteen-month-old had found a way to escape. He'd been working hard on the project lately, but she'd thought she would notice if he...

Her heart was beating quickly, like a bird flapping in her chest, but she still wasn't panicked. He had to be close by. She'd seen him only a minute ago.

The customer tried to hand her his money to pay for the

German Chocolate cake she'd boxed for him, but she didn't even notice, brushing right past him, leaving her booth along the side of the street unattended without a second thought. She had to find Kevin.

The Thursday San Rey Farmers' Market was popular and people filled the closed-off street, milling back and forth in clumps, making it very hard to see a pint-size child wandering between the legs of the adults.

"Have you seen Kevin?" Jolene called to her friend and roommate Mandy Jensen who ran the soft pretzel machine.

"Kevin?" Mandy looked up and down the banner-filled street. Booths selling everything from freshly picked arugula to wildly painted garden elves met her gaze, but no little boy. "No, I thought you had him in the playpen."

"I thought so, too," Jolene called back, but she was already hurrying, rushing, and panic was beginning to lap at the edges of her sense of control. Her long, blond braid hit her back as she went, bouncing off one shoulder and then another as she turned her head to search out every cranny she came upon.

"Have you seen a little blond boy coming by here?" she asked a complete stranger, not waiting for an answer when the woman looked at her blankly. Turning, she ran to the other side of the street. "Have you seen a little boy?" she called out. "My little boy is missing. Please, please, have you seen him?"

Someone grabbed her arm and she turned to see that it was Mandy.

"I'll take this end of the street," her friend told her, waving back toward the center of town. "You go the way you're going. We'll find him, Jolene. Don't you worry."

"Don't you worry, don't you worry." The words pounded in her head but she couldn't quite grasp what they meant, because worried was all she was right now. Kevin, his sweet little face, his huge blue eyes, his devilish smile, his fat little legs...

"He's wearing blue overalls and a red checkered shirt," she called out to anyone who would listen as she began to run. "He's got to be here somewhere. Have you seen a little boy?"

People looked up, surprised, as she passed, at first not understanding, but looking sympathetic once they realized what was going on. But no one had seen him. How could that be? She wanted to shake someone. Someone had to have seen him. He didn't just disappear. How could he have come down this entire street and no one notice?

"Kevin!" she called out, her voice almost breaking with despair. "Kevin, where are you?" There was a frantic fear growing in the pit of her stomach, a feeling only a mother could know. My God, where was he?

If asked, Grant Fargo would have admitted he didn't know much about little kids. The only child he'd been close to at all was his brother's little girl, Allison, and she was eleven now. He could hardly remember when she'd been a toddler. At any rate, though he was no expert, as he watched the little blond boy approach, he had a pretty good idea that a child this size shouldn't be wandering the streets by himself. There must be someone nearby attached to him, he reasoned. Some mother or baby-sitter would show up at any moment. So he didn't pay too much attention as the kid climbed up on the stone bench beside him and began eyeing the cookie he was eating.

"Hi," he said to him at last, brushing a few dry crumbs from the fine Italian fabric of his suit pants leg. "What's your name?"

No response. But there was a glint in the blue eyes.

"You want one of these cookies, don't you?" Grant said

conversationally. He patted the waxed paper bag beside him, tempted to offer a snack to the child, but then thought twice and hesitated. "Listen, I'd give you one, but I don't think your mom would like it." He held up the cookie he'd had a bite of and studied it. "You see, moms have this thing about their kids taking food from strangers...."

Too late he learned a lesson about eighteen-month-old baby boys. They have no manners and they seldom wait to be invited to take a snack that appeals to them. One chubby little arm shot out and four fingers and a thumb plunged into the bag, grabbed hold of a cookie and shot out again. The boy gave Grant a triumphant grin and clamped down on the cookie with all four teeth.

"Hey." Grant glared at him, his straight, dark brows adding a stern look to his classically handsome face. He didn't remember Allison ever acting like this. "You'd better not eat that. Before you know it, we'll have your mother coming after me with a lawsuit for poisoning her son." He reached out and tried to pry the cookie from the child. "Come on," he ordered in a tone that indicated he was used to having orders obeyed. "Give it back."

It was surprising that a kid could let out such a loud shriek when his mouth was clamped down tightly around a cookie. But that was exactly what happened. A siren from a passing fire engine couldn't have caused more commotion. People stopped dead and turned to look.

"Why, look at that man," declared a short, redheaded woman, frowning. "He's taking a cookie away from that poor child."

Hearing her, Grant looked up and attempted a smile, though he was still tugging on the cookie. He tried to explain.

"No, listen, it's my cookie. I mean, it's not his. I mean..."

The redheaded woman would have none of it. She stood before the two of them with her hands on her hips. "Why, the selfishness. I never heard of such a thing before."

The cookie crumbled, as cookies are wont to do, and Grant drew back a handful of crumbs. More crumbs covered the bright red little face of the still shrieking child and Grant hesitated, wanting to stop the noise but wanting to explain himself to the redheaded woman and her silver-haired companion who had just arrived on the scene at the same time.

"Look, I don't know this child," he began, waving his hand to try to get rid of the crumbs. "I never saw him before in my life and…"

"Then why were you forcing him to eat that cookie?" the silver-haired woman demanded. Having come upon the scene late and noting the crumbs on the boy's face, she'd made a quick assumption. She turned, surveying the still-gathering crowd. "Force-feeding a child. Outrageous." Her glare was ferocious. "I think it's time to go to the police," she informed her friend.

Grant blinked and shook his head as though he could clear it of this nightmare if he only shook hard enough. "No, wait. I'm trying to explain…"

But before he could, Jolene Campbell emerged from a knot of people, saw her son and cried out, rushing to him.

"Oh, Kevin!" she cried, grabbing him up into her arms and holding him tightly. "Kevin, Kevin, Kevin," she muttered, tears welling in her eyes and relief making her dizzy. "Baby, baby."

"See, here's his mom," Grant said, gesturing for the benefit of the two women who still seemed to hold him in contempt of some detail of social etiquette he hadn't quite figured out yet. "Now everything will be okay."

But the silver-haired woman seemed to think her duty as

monitor of what went on in the streets of her town was not yet fulfilled. Stepping forward, she tapped Jolene on the shoulder.

"My dear, is this your child?" she said, still glaring at Grant. "I just think you should know. That man was forcing him to eat cookies just now. I don't know what he thought he was doing, but the boy was struggling like anything. Honest."

Grant rose, clutching his bag of cookies, hoping to make a quick getaway, but Jolene whirled and stared at him, her silver eyes huge in wonder. "Why would you do that?" she asked him.

Grant met her gaze and paused, startled by her beautiful eyes. At first glance, they seemed too silver to be real, filled with shooting stars that were only emphasized by the thick golden lashes that framed them. "What is she, a witch?" his mind whispered to him, but that was hardly relevant to the situation and he shook the thought away. Instead he eyed his escape route and tried to answer at the same time.

"No, I wasn't trying to make him eat it. You don't understand. I was trying to get the cookie away from him."

"You see?" crowed the redhead, rolling her eyes. "Talk about taking candy from the mouths of babes. And look. He's got a whole bag of them. You'd think he could have spared just one for the kid. Really, some people."

Grant groaned and Jolene frowned, looking from the woman to Grant and back again, not sure what to make of these claims. Her child was hugging her neck with both arms, but his head was turned and he was watching Grant as well. Grant caught the look. There was something about the glint in his round baby eyes....

"Here," Grant muttered, thrusting the bag of cookies into Jolene's hand. This was a no-win situation and he'd had enough of it. "Take them. Throw them away or eat them, I don't care." He began to back away, holding his hands up as though someone had a gun up against his spine. "I didn't try to force him to eat a cookie. I was trying to take it away because I thought you wouldn't want him taking food from a stranger. That was it, lady. Honest."

"Wait," she said, taking a step toward him. "I wasn't accusing you..."

But he didn't wait. Instead he turned on his heel and melted into the crowd.

Jolene stared after him, more confused than ever. But she had her baby in her arms, and that was all she really cared about. "Come on, Kev," she said, kissing his fat baby cheek, even though crumbs of cookie still remained. "Let's go back to the booth."

People made way for her and she smiled her gratitude, full of relief that everything was turning out fine after all. It wasn't until she was back at her pastry booth, dropping her son into his playpen once again and looking for a way to fortify its security, that she realized she still had the bag of cookies clutched in her hand. That made her think of the handsome man who'd given them to her, but she pushed the thought away. Whatever the man had been up to, she would never see him again, so it hardly mattered. She had Kevin back, safe and sound, and that was all she cared about.

Two

The Farmers' Market was held every Thursday and Jolene never missed one. Selling her baked goods here was her main means of support. Driving in from the apartment she shared with Mandy, a week after the runaway incident, this time she came prepared with a borrowed old-fashioned wooden playpen that was sure to keep Kevin in one spot.

"Okay my little caged bird," she muttered as she gave him a last hug before getting to work, stroking the downy blond pelt that covered his round little head. "You've got twenty-five toys in here with you. Plenty to do. No running away. You hear?"

He cooed happily, but as she drew back, she noticed that his gaze was on something over her shoulder and his mouth had fallen open in a perfect O.

"Cookie!" he cried, thrusting out his fat little fist.

Rising, she turned to find the man from the week before standing at the counter watching her exchange with her son.

"You again," she said, gazing at him curiously.

"Yes, it's me." He smiled at her a bit ruefully, then waved at Kevin. "Hi, kid," he said softly. "How are you doing?"

Kevin made a sound that bore a strong resemblance to a Bronx cheer, but Jolene didn't notice. Her bright eyes narrowed as she looked Grant over, taking his measure. He was a handsome man with a sense of humor shining in his eyes. The smile he gave her was infectious, a fact that immediately made her wary. She didn't trust men who smiled too easily.

Behind the smile, beware the guile. That had been one of her grandmother's favorite sayings, and Jolene had once ignored it and paid the price.

But she had to admit, this man didn't look threatening. He was probably in his thirties, but his face had a boyish look that was immediately endearing. His nicely tailored suit was just saved from looking too formal for this scene by the casual air of assurance he wore with it, and she was suddenly aware of the contrast she made in her crisp jeans and plaid shirt, the tails tied into a knot just above the waist. The Daisy Mae braids didn't do much to help her look sophisticated, either.

Dogpatch meets Madison Avenue, she thought, laughing at herself.

"What can I do for you?" she asked, hanging back a bit. She had no reason to think badly of him, but what had happened last week had been a little strange. He smiled at her, his white teeth gleaming in the morning sunlight, making her blink.

Women usually melt when he smiles like that, she thought to herself. *That's what he does it for.* But she wouldn't. No way. She'd been through the fires and come out stronger than most.

"I came by to make sure the child was all right," he told her. It sounded nice, sounded caring, but it was a complete lie.

He often came by the Farmers' Market on Thursdays to search out something unusual the gourmet farmers might have brought to town. As owner and manager of a restaurant that prided itself on being ahead of the trends, he liked to be on the lookout for what was developing, poised to be the first to notice, and this was a good place to explore for possibilities. He'd been walking down the street, checking out the marketplace as he usually did on Thursdays, and suddenly there she'd been. It hadn't occurred to him before that she might be a vendor here. He couldn't imagine how he could have avoided noticing her on previous visits.

But in the moment he'd seen her, his first impulse had been to turn and go another way. If it hadn't been for those strange and beautiful eyes, he probably would have done exactly that. Anything to avoid another encounter with the child from…well, maybe hell was a bit strong. The child from mischief-land, at least.

But he smiled and went on with the masquerade. "I felt badly about what happened last week and I wanted to make sure you understood I didn't do anything to the boy."

She nodded slowly. "He's fine. There's no need for you to worry."

"Uh, good. I'm glad to hear that." Grant hesitated, then held out his hand. "My name's Grant Fargo," he told her. "And yours is…?"

She really didn't want to tell him, but there didn't seem to be any way to avoid it. "Jolene Campbell," she said.

"Nice to meet you, Jolene."

She nodded solemnly, not conceding anything.

His attention was centered on her eyes and she looked away with a gesture of impatience, denying them to him, turning to the side. It always started this way. She was going to have to start wearing sunglasses so that she could get on with her life without all these interruptions. There were things to do and she meant to get them done.

Ignoring his presence, she began to pry open the large cardboard boxes she'd used to cart her wares in from the parking lot to her booth. The boxes were filled with pastries she'd been up most of the night baking. She began to take them out one by one, filling the display case with the ones that didn't need refrigeration. But all the time, she could see him out of the corner of her gaze and she knew he wasn't going anywhere.

"You know, your eyes—they're really strange."

He said it as though he'd just discovered something he was sure no one else had ever noticed before. As though it would be news to her. She paused and drummed her fingers on the counter. Talk about her eyes was old hat. She'd heard it all before. Too many times.

But he wasn't going to let it go. "Your eyes. They're just so…so…"

She raised her gaze to meet his, giving him the full treatment and watching him react with a wonder mixed with impatience. It was odd what her eyes sometimes did to people. They felt like normal eyes to her, but most passersby did a double take when they noticed them. She'd gone through periods where she'd cursed having such attention getters, and gone through periods where she'd been downright proud she was different in some way. Lately she'd just been bored with the whole thing. She had a life to live and attention to her unique eyes got in the way.

She watched as he struggled for words to describe them. "All-seeing?" she suggested, only slightly sarcastic. "All-knowing?"

He frowned, his face quite serious as he studied her. "No, that's not it."

Her wide mouth quirked at the corners. At least he wasn't merely pandering. "Eerie? Outlandish? Creepy?" This was actually starting to be fun as his expressive face reacted to each word she threw out. "Otherworldly?"

"No. Not exactly." He was shaking his head, his straight, dark brows drawn together in concentration.

She widened her eyes dramatically and batted the lashes. "Spooky?" she guessed.

He shook his head. "No, not at all. They're quite beautiful. They...they give me shivers."

He wasn't kidding. There was something in his tone, something in the light in *his* eyes, that caught her up short. He had the look of someone who'd just seen something that had touched him, found a chord in his soul and elicited a response, like someone who'd heard a beautiful piece of classical music that had surprised him by sending emotion slicing through him.

Their gazes seemed to lock, and things on the street behind them seemed to fade and run like watercolors. She felt funny, light-headed, and she shook herself, as though to bring back reality.

"What?" he said, looking at her strangely.

"I didn't say anything," she told him, trying very hard to frown. She stared at him for a beat too long, then recovered her senses and made an impatient gesture meant to encourage him to move on.

"Look, I'm really going to be busy here in a few minutes, and I need to get things ready. So if you don't mind..."

"No, I don't mind," he murmured, but his words didn't really make any sense.

She hesitated, then turned from him and set up her cash

box, determined to ignore him if he wouldn't go away. And for the first time, he seemed to rouse himself from his trance, to take in the booth and the baked items she'd been arranging on her counter.

"What's all this?" he asked, blinking as though he'd just woken up.

She put her hands on her hips and swept the counter with an evaluating glance and began a catalog. "Bear claws. German Chocolate cake. Almond cookies..."

"I know, I know." He gave the items another look, then met her gaze. "What I mean is, where did you get these pastries? They look great."

She shrugged and said simply, "I made them."

He frowned. "You?"

That certainly set her teeth on edge. This was what she hated about men. It happened every time. Just because she had what many considered a pretty face and a pleasing figure and those startling eyes—just because she was a blonde—it always seemed to come as a total surprise to men that she might have a talent or two up her sleeve. Sometimes she thought they actually resented it—as though she were supposed to concentrate on being attractive and leave the hard work to the homely chicks. Her jaw set. For a moment she'd thought he might be different. Wrong again.

"Yes, me," she said, barely holding back the impulse to snap. "All by myself in my own little apartment kitchen."

"You're kidding." He gazed at the wares before him and his eyes narrowed thoughtfully. "If you can do this in a little kitchen," he murmured almost to himself. "Imagine what you could do with commercial ovens at your disposal."

She blinked. Just when she'd been ready to pigeonhole him, he'd surprised her again. She hesitated and shrugged.

If he was interested in bakery items, far be it from her to discourage him. Customers were what she lived for.

"Would you like to try one?" she asked.

"Yes, I would," he said, reaching for his wallet. "Let's see…how about a slice of cheesecake. And a Napoleon. And one of those cherry tarts."

She blinked and started to laugh. "All three?"

He grinned and nodded as though he were glad she was showing signs that she might warm up eventually. "All three."

She shrugged, amused but at a loss. "Do you want me to box them?"

He shook his head. "No, I'll try them here. Put them on separate plates, please."

Now she was completely confused. It seemed a little early in the morning for gluttony, and he really didn't seem the type. Then a possible answer occurred to her.

"Oh, do you have friends with you?" she asked, craning to look behind him. There were others on the street. The place was beginning to come to life. But there was no one who looked as though he or she belonged to this strange man.

"No," he said, confirming her original judgment. "There's only me."

She raised an eyebrow. "Oh."

The man wanted three pastries and that was what he should have. She glanced back to make sure Kevin was busily playing with his blocks, then pulled out three paper plates and went to work, picking out nice specimens and setting all three plates on a tray. He put a few bills down on the counter and took the tray from her, murmuring his thanks. Taking the plastic fork she'd provided, he took a bite of the cheesecake and rolled it around on his tongue. She leaned back against a stack of boxes with her arms folded, watching curiously, as his eyes seemed to get a very distant look. Either the man loved cheesecake or he was a very discerning connoisseur.

When the bite was finished, he prodded the confection with the fork, examining the crust, mashing the creamy center through the tines in a way that made her wince. Then he turned to the Napoleon and did the same to it before popping a large bite into his mouth.

She frowned, toying with the idea of saying something to him about his unusual way of eating, but before she had a chance, Kevin threw a block out of the playpen and she bent to retrieve it. When she rose again, she turned and found the man breaking apart the cherry tart as though he might find something sinister hidden in its depths. She handed the block to her son absently, frowning as she watched the man put a taste of the tart in his mouth and narrow his eyes. He looked as though he were listening to something she couldn't quite hear, and as she watched, she had to hold back a flash of annoyance.

What the heck was he doing, anyway? Didn't he have any respect for decent food? She bit her tongue. After all, he'd bought the pastries. She had no right to complain about the way he ate them. But she didn't like it. She didn't like it at all.

Oblivious to her emotions, he looked at her again, nodded with a trace of a smile and put the plate down, reaching for a napkin. "Thanks," he said as he wiped away a few crumbs. "Great stuff."

She stepped forward and looked at the tray in dismay. He'd had one bite of each and done a lot of damage along the way. "That's it? You're not going to finish them?"

He let out a short laugh. "Are you kidding? I'd turn into a bowling ball if I ate whole portions." He tossed his napkin into her trash can.

"Listen, I work with food. I have to test it all the time. And I've got to say, these are some darn good pastries."

She looked from him to the demolished plates again, still at sea. "I...I'm glad you like them."

He nodded, thinking. "I do." He looked her up and down, assessing more than her baking abilities. A smile lit his eyes and he nodded as though agreeing with something he'd just thought of. "Listen, how would you like to come work for me?"

"For you?" She drew back suspiciously. She hadn't expected anything like this. "Doing what?"

"Believe it or not, I need a pastry chef." He pulled out his wallet again and found a business card to show her. "I've got a restaurant, the Max Grill in Pasadena. Our pastry chef quit last month and we've been making do with a local bakery." He gestured toward her wares. "I like what you've got here. How about giving it a try?"

She studied the card to keep from meeting his gaze. The Max Grill. She'd heard of it, though she'd never eaten there. Her budget ran more to fast-food hamburger stands.

"I don't think so," she told him, holding the card out to him. "Thanks anyway."

He smiled at her, bemused. She didn't trust him. He could see it in her spectacular eyes, sense it in her body language. He'd never seen anyone like her before and he had an instinctive feeling that he shouldn't let her slip out of his life without at least thinking it over.

"Listen, just come by one day this week and take a look at our setup," he suggested, avoiding taking back the card. "I think you'll like what you see."

She was shaking her head, but he didn't let her get a word in. "I've got two big commercial baking ovens. They can be yours every morning. Just think of the things you could try there that you've never been able to do before."

His smile was contagious. "Come on by and give us a chance. And after you fall in love with the place, we'll talk. We'll negotiate your salary. I pay pretty decently." He jerked his head toward the playpen. "You might even be able to afford to get a baby-sitter for the kid."

Her head snapped around and she gazed at him levelly. Baby-sitting for her kid, indeed! As if she would let anyone else raise her child for her. Wasn't that just like a man? Suddenly it all seemed much too familiar. Sure, get the kid out of the way so they could get to know each other better. Where had she ever heard that before?

"I'm afraid I can't help you out," she said stiffly, dropping the card into her trash, since he wouldn't take it back.

He watched her defiant gesture with a slight frown. "You won't even come take a look at the place?"

She held her head high and gazed at him across the bridge of her nose. "No."

His frown deepened. "Do you have some other job? Besides this, I mean."

He was awfully persistent and she looked toward where Mandy was selling pretzels to a young boy. She might have to call for reinforcements if he kept this up. "Let's just say my family obligations rule it out."

His face cleared. "Ah, I see. Your husband wouldn't approve?"

She merely smiled, and just as she'd suspected, his eyes clouded over and he seemed to lose interest fast. She'd seen him look at her empty ring finger before and he did so again now. But he shrugged and began to back away.

"Well, in that case," he said smoothly. "I won't bother you any further."

She opened her mouth to say something else, but he was already turning from her and she couldn't remember what it was going to be anyway. She watched him stop by

Mandy's pretzel stand and buy one of the twisted pieces of bread. She was tempted to take offense when she noticed him munching on it. After all, he hadn't finished her pastries, had he?

Hey, stop it, she scolded herself immediately. *If you're going to be jealous of something like that, you might as well give it up.*

He turned and caught her watching, waved the pretzel at her and started off, while she flushed, wishing she'd turned away sooner. Clenching her jaw with new determination, she went back to setting up her counter, carefully avoiding a look in his direction again and a moment later, Mandy hurried over.

"What happened?" she asked, her eyes bright. "That man I just sold a pretzel to—he was over here talking to you forever. What did he want?"

Jolene looked up at her friend and roommate and sighed. "What do you think? He actually thought I would fall for the old offer of a job trick. He said he ran a restaurant and needed a pastry chef. Can you believe it?"

Mandy frowned, considering carefully. "You turned him down?"

"I had to."

"Why?"

Jolene put a stack of napkins into the holder before answering. "Because he's a guy." She glanced at her friend, then toward her child. "And I know all about guys. I've been down that road before."

"I know, but..." Mandy frowned, biting her lip.

She tried another vein, hoping to make it clear. "You should have seen how quickly he backed off once he thought I was married."

Mandy's frown only deepened. "But you're not married."

Jolene pushed her hair back impatiently, turning away. No, she wasn't married. But she might as well be. "I know that," she said quickly. "But he doesn't. And once he heard that, he was out of here like a shot."

Mandy raised one dark eyebrow, surveying her friend with a glint of amusement. "Maybe he's a gentleman."

"What?" Jolene gave her an outlandish look. Gentlemen didn't hang around offering jobs that didn't exist.

But Mandy smiled, liking her idea. "Sure. Once he found out you were already spoken for, he decided to back off." She gave her friend a teasing grin. "He just couldn't bear to tempt himself any further."

Jolene threw up her hands. "Oh, *puhlease*, Mandy," she said, though she had to admit, in her secret heart, such a scenario pleased her, too.

Mandy shook her head and flopped down on the camp stool Jolene kept behind the counter. "Well, there's only one problem with your theory. In point of fact, he asked me if you were married. And since I didn't know you were giving him that impression on purpose, I told him the truth."

The two friends stared at each other, then both started to laugh.

"Oh, brother, now I feel like an idiot," Jolene admitted, shaking her head. Her attempt at a tough shell had melted away in an instant. It hadn't been a very comfortable fit anyway.

"So I guess maybe his job offer was on the level," Mandy suggested.

Jolene shrugged. "Maybe." But she turned away and began another chore, as though it hardly mattered in the end.

Mandy was silent for a while, but finally blurted out, "You're nuts. You know very well we're not making it.

The rent is eating up all the money we make here. We need something else.''

Jolene winced, knowing her words were true enough, but hating to face facts just yet. "All we need is a couple of good days..."

"A couple won't do it," Mandy told her bluntly. "A month of good days might get us by. You've got Kevin. We've both got the rent to pay and food to buy. We've got to do something to get more cash coming in. I'm thinking about going back to the factory...."

Jolene spun to face her friend. "Oh, Mandy, no. You hated that place."

Mandy shrugged, and Jolene knew her friend was fighting back tears. She had hated the factory, though she'd been a supervisor. The place had been a garment shop, full of immigrants who couldn't get anything better, and the boss had pushed her to push them to the limit. Jolene knew Mandy would rather do almost anything else than go back there. Still, it was pretty clear they weren't making it the way things were going now.

"I don't know what else to do," Mandy said softly.

The two of them had met a year before when Mandy had moved her pretzel machine next to Jolene's booth. They'd quickly become good friends and they'd moved in together to save rent money from overwhelming them. Mandy was wonderful with Kevin and the three of them formed a nice little family. The only fly in the ointment so far had been Mandy's boyfriend, Stan. Try as she would, Jolene just couldn't hit it off with him and she really resented the way he treated Mandy. But his photography business had really picked up in the past few months, leaving him less time to hang around their apartment, so the waters were a bit calmer.

However, she had to admit it was time to face facts. They

weren't making enough money to make it from month to month. Something would have to be done. Jolene looked at Mandy's miserable face and she threw her arms around her. "We'll think of something," she said, the urge to comfort sounding just a little desperate. "Just give it a few more days. Something will come up. It has to."

Mandy shook her head. "It hasn't so far. We've got to do something. And we've got to do it now."

Jolene closed her eyes and hugged her friend more tightly. The image of Grant Fargo swam into her mind and she sighed. It was too bad he was so attractive. And it was very lucky such things didn't get to her these days. She'd learned her lessons early and she knew what it was like to steel herself against temptation.

"Okay," she said, her shoulders sagging. "I'll think about it. But I'm not promising anything."

Kevin, ignored too long, let out a shriek and both women turned toward him.

"They certainly start at a young age, don't they?" Mandy muttered. And both women laughed.

Three

Grant took in the banquet room at a glance. Decorated for a baby shower, pink and blue teddy bears floated down from the ceiling and fluffy white swans cruised down the center of the long table. He nodded approvingly.

"You did a great job putting this together," he told the tall, elegant woman standing beside him.

"Thank you, boss," Michelle answered gravely, her green eyes and carefully coiffed auburn hair advertising her Irish heritage. "We aim to please."

He laughed. "You aim to take over the world, and we all know it," he teased her. "I keep thinking I'll walk in here some morning and find out you now hold the papers on the place."

Her smile was pleased, but she demurred. "You know I wouldn't do that without consulting you first," she teased back.

His answering grin faded as his thoughts took in their

past together. "You're a good friend, Michelle. You know I never would have made a success of this place without you," he told her solemnly. "Without you and Tony giving me moral support when our dad died, I never would have taken this on. I wouldn't have had the guts."

She smiled and patted his arm. "Don't exaggerate, darling," she told him in a motherly tone. "You always had more guts than all the rest of us put together." She shook her head when he looked about to speak and turned to another topic. "By the way," she mentioned casually. "How is your brother these days?"

"Tony?" Grant gave a quick thought to his once irascible older sibling. "Tony, as usual, could use a life."

Michelle flashed a smile in his direction, but she didn't pause as she counted out the change for the cash register. "Couldn't we all?" she murmured.

He leaned against the counter, watching her with a thoughtful frown. "No, I really mean it about Tony. You and me, Michelle, we're not the marrying kind. We've been there and done that and learned to avoid it. We know how to have our fun without entanglements and commitments. But Tony..." He grimaced. "Well, he's got the kid and all and it's making him nutty. He's like a mother hen these days." His frown deepened as he remembered his brother coming to the door in an apron with huge red apples painted all over it the last time he'd appeared unannounced at his door. "Damn it all, he needs a wife."

Michelle nodded as she filled a bin with nickels, putting them in neat stacks. "Is there anyone on the horizon right now?" she asked him.

Grant shook his head. "Naw. He doesn't even date. His whole life is wrapped up in his daughter, Allison. Ever since Mary died..." He glanced at Michelle, aware that he was treading on dangerous ground when criticizing his brother's response to his wife's death two years before. "Well, for the first year or so, you could understand it. I mean, Mary was wonderful and I think, if he hadn't had Allison to take care of, he might have died, too. You know? His life just seemed to come to a stop."

Michelle's green eyes clouded. "Yes," she said softly. "I remember."

Grant nodded. "But now it's time to move on. He needs a new woman in his life. That would turn things around, get him back in gear. If only I could find him someone..." His eyes brightened. "You know, I saw this girl the other day..." His voice trailed off as he thought of her.

Michelle looked up curiously. "What girl?"

"Hmm?" He met her gaze and realized he'd left her hanging. "Oh, this girl at the Farmers' Market. I tried to hire her as a pastry chef but she turned me down." He nodded slowly, thinking hard and coming to a decision. "You know, now that I think about it, she'd be perfect for Tony."

"Who? This girl at the Farmers' Market?"

"Why didn't I realize this before?" He grew more excited about the idea as more details came to him. "She's cuter than heck and she can cook and she's got a kid, too."

"Grant..."

He threw out his arms, amazed at how obligingly accommodating life could be. "I mean, how perfect can you get? They could have one of those...what do you call them? Blended families."

Michelle laughed, looking as though she was tempted to give his dark hair an affectionate ruffle. Luckily she held back the impulse, but her tone was teasing. "Whoa there, pardner. Don't you think you're getting the cart before the horse? They haven't even met yet and you've got them knitting booties together."

He gazed at her earnestly. "What do you think, Michelle? What would happen if I tried a little matchmaking? Come on, you know Tony almost as well as I do. What do you think?"

Michelle hesitated, shaking her head as she studied his face. "I knew Tony once," she admitted softly. "But ever since he came back from college with Mary on his arm..."

"Oh, come on. That was years ago."

She raised a wise eyebrow. "Exactly my point."

She began refilling saltcellars on the tables and he followed her, reaching out to open one for her. "So he got married and broke up that old gang of ours," he murmured, handing her the empty container. "That doesn't erase all those years growing up in the canyon and chasing each other around Lincoln Elementary."

She turned to go to the next table, but a smile was beginning to tease the corners of her mouth.

He noted it and grinned, adding another recollection he knew she would share. "Or going to Mary Engle's birthday party and ending up in her fishpond."

She managed to force back her giggle but she couldn't resist adding her own memory. "Or taking the bus down Lake Avenue from Eliot Junior High to go to the Rose Bowl Café for orange freezes," she remembered reluctantly as she poured out another stream of white crystals.

He nodded his approval as he dropped into a chair right under where she was working. He had her now. He was going to need some expert female advice if he were going to match his brother up with a wife, and Michelle was the best manipulator he knew. "Or ditching high school," he went on, adding another memory to lure her in, "piling into Tony's old Chevy and heading down to Chavez Ravine to watch the Dodgers play in the World Series."

"Gosh, we really did have fun in those days," Michelle

agreed, smiling broadly at last. Looking down at him, she shook her head. "Remember the beach parties at Laguna?"

He nodded and rose, snagging a thorn-shaved white rose from the vase on the table and tucking it behind her ear. "Cruising Hollywood Boulevard with a car full of kids on a Saturday night?"

She grinned, touching the rose but leaving it where he'd put it. "Staying up all night on the sidewalk on New Year's Eve to watch the Rose Parade?"

"And falling asleep before it came?"

They both laughed.

"The all-night gab sessions in your backyard?" he added.

"The proms at the Huntington Sheraton?" she chimed in, eyes narrowing as she remembered her slinky black velvet prom dress.

"It's a Ritz-Carleton now."

She frowned and waved as though to push reality away. "Don't tell me that. I'm floating in the past."

He sank into a chair at the table where they'd had lunch together and motioned for her to join him. "Well, float yourself over here and tell me what you think about my idea."

She came, sliding in beside him, but her eyes didn't smile. "To find Tony a mate?"

"Yeah."

She looked him over with quiet affection. "If this person is so perfect, why don't you snap her up yourself?" she asked him. "It's about time you started getting serious again, don't you think?"

Grant grimaced and looked away. Michelle was being very delicate and discreet. She hadn't even mentioned Stephanie's name. In fact, he didn't think anyone in his family or circle of friends had mentioned her name since the divorce. Everyone assumed that the way she'd left had hurt him so badly, he couldn't stand to be reminded. And for once, everyone was pretty much right.

Turning back, he flashed his friend a brilliant smile. "How can you say something like that? I thought you knew me better. I'm never serious."

She covered his hand with her own and gave it a squeeze. "Maybe you should be," she suggested softly.

He shook his head. "Not now. One Fargo brother at a time. And right now, I'm working on Tony. We've got to get him hitched."

Michelle sat back and rolled her eyes. "I think you'd better forget it," she advised. "If he figures out what you're doing, he'll kill you."

He waved a forefinger at her. "Ah, but that's the heart of the matter, isn't it? I'll be subtle. I'll be tactful. I'll masterfully manipulate events. He'll never know what I'm doing until it's too late."

Michelle laughed, her white teeth glistening behind the slick Persian melon lipstick that was her trademark. The thought of this open-faced man pulling the wool over his brother's eyes boggled the mind.

But before she could explain to him just how crazy this was, she saw his eyes change and saw him start to his feet, muttering, "My God, I can't believe it," and she turned to see a pretty young woman picking her way through the darkened restaurant, looking nervously from one side to the other.

Grant started toward her but Michelle followed more slowly. The woman was young, probably in her late twenties, and yet she had a youthful air that made her seem years younger. She was dressed in designer jeans and a pink sweater and her hair was in braids. This had to be the pretty pastry chef, and though she hid it behind a pleasant smile, unease hovered at the back of Michelle's eyes. Here she was, the girl Grant had earmarked for Tony. Things were moving more quickly than she could have anticipated.

Jolene wasn't sure what she was doing here. She'd turned a deaf ear to Mandy's persuasion for two days, but this morning, when Kevin had banged his cup for orange juice and she'd heard herself explaining to him that there wouldn't be enough money to buy things like that until after next Thursday, she'd realized she was just being stubborn. If the man needed a pastry chef, why not take the job? If it turned out her first instincts were right and he only wanted a date for the evening—well, if she could walk in, she could walk out. She was a grown woman. She ought to be able to handle it.

So here she was in this restaurant located at the edge of Old Town. It seemed nice enough. A decorator had worked hard to achieve just the right Southwestern flair. A large saguaro cactus stood brooding in the entryway and red tiles stretched as far as the eye could see. Desert palms appeared in clumps here and there, hiding tables and supply cabinets, and Mexican ceramics sat propped against faux-Navajo rugs.

There was someone working behind the bar and she started toward it, but before she got there, Grant appeared out of nowhere, heading her off at the pass.

"Hi," he said, smiling at her, his gorgeous dark eyes shining. "I'm glad you decided to come take a look at us."

She came to a stop, feeling just a bit awkward. A tall, elegant woman was walking up behind him and she glanced at her with a quick smile, then looked back at Grant.

"Is the job still open?" Jolene asked him abruptly.

He nodded, trying to stay serious but having a hard time hiding his reaction to her surprise arrival. "I've been holding it for you," he fibbed, because after all, there hadn't been any other applicants.

"I didn't say I'd take it," she said hastily. "I just wanted to check it out and see..."

He shrugged his casual acceptance. "No problem. You'll like it here." Turning, he deftly included Michelle. "This is my assistant manager, Michelle Gleason. And your name is again...?"

It gave her a start to realize he didn't remember her name. "Jolene Campbell," she said, holding out her hand to the woman for a quick acknowledgment.

"Jolene makes some nice pastries," Grant went on, looking her over as though he were very pleased she'd come, but talking to Michelle. "If she approves of the terms, I'm thinking of offering her a six month contract to start with."

"A real contract?" Jolene asked, though that was just a ploy to give her time to think and she didn't wait for an answer. "I don't know about that. I thought maybe I could just bring over some of the things I baked each day and you could choose what might fit your needs...."

He was shaking his head and her voice trailed off. Obviously that was not what he'd had in mind.

"I've got to have a full-time pastry chef," he told her. "I'd want you to do your baking here."

She grimaced, looking around at the tables standing in wait for a flood of customers later on in the afternoon.

"You see, that's going to be a problem," she said, her tone confident. The only evidence of the nervousness she felt was her hand playing with the tassles on her purse. "Tell you the truth, I sort of bake what I feel like baking when I feel like it. If I was under contract..."

"We're not all that rigid here. You'll be free to do a lot of experimenting." He smiled at her, and she had a quick impression of being coaxed, beguiled. He really wanted her to take this job. She frowned, wondering why.

But he didn't notice. "Come on back to the kitchen," he said, turning. "I'll show you around."

She glanced at Michelle, then back at Grant. "Okay," she said. "I'd like to see it."

He was proud of his place and it showed. And she had to hand it to him, he had something to be proud of. The kitchen gleamed with stainless-steel efficiency. She hadn't seen such impressive equipment since culinary school. Her heart beat a little faster as she took it all in. It would be very different to do her baking in a place like this.

"What sort of food do you serve?" she asked, though she thought she probably knew.

"California modern."

She glanced at him as she let her hand trail along the cool surface of a stainless-steel counter. "Trendy stuff?"

He shrugged, his hands in his pockets. "I guess you could call it that."

She wrinkled her nose, looking at him candidly. "I'm not much for trendy stuff. I don't follow trends myself."

He grinned at her. "Just a sweet old-fashioned girl?"

Her chin rose. "Do you have something against traditions?"

"No, not at all."

"Good." She sighed softly. She was going to take the job. There really were no more excuses not to. Just one little item had to be cleared up first. "I'd need to bring my little boy to work with me," she told him, turning her head so that she could judge his reaction. "Could you handle that?"

His face said it all, but that was hardly necessary to interpret, because his words did the job on their own. "No way. This is a place of business. We can't have kids running around."

She smiled, almost relieved. "Then you won't have me running around, either," she said firmly, turning to go.

"Wait." He stood in her way. "Now don't be so hasty. Maybe we can work something out."

She glanced into his eyes. There it was again, the sense that he was just a little too anxious to have her here. "There's nothing to work out," she said firmly. "Either Kevin comes with me or I don't come. I won't leave him with a baby-sitter. The most important thing I have to do with my life is to raise him. I won't leave it to someone else."

He looked pained, torn. "I don't know how we can manage that. Insurance…safety considerations…"

Suddenly Michelle interposed herself with quiet dignity, one hand on Grant's arm. "We'll manage," she said firmly, smiling at Jolene.

Grant looked at her and blinked. "We'll manage?" he echoed.

She nodded. "Leave it to me," she said.

He hesitated a moment, but something in Michelle's eyes told him to agree or face the consequences. Smiling, he gave in. "We'll manage," he told Jolene with a disarming shrug. "Somehow."

Jolene didn't have time to marvel on the interplay between the two of them, and the influence the woman seemed to have over Grant. He grabbed her hand and started toward his office at the corner of the wide room.

"Come on, I want to sign you up before you have a chance to think of any other roadblocks."

She had a quick glimpse of Michelle's face and the distinct impression that the woman would have liked to have come along with them, but Grant moved quickly and made it pretty clear he wanted to be alone with Jolene for the moment. She hesitated at the door wondering what this woman knew that she didn't—and should. But Grant still had hold of her hand and he tugged, pulling her into the office and shutting the door behind her.

"Sit down," he told her, pointing to a chair across the desk from where he settled. "We should get to know each other."

She sat gingerly on the edge of the chair. "I don't know why," she countered. "I'm not applying to be your friend. Just your pastry chef."

He looked surprised, then laughed. "You got me there," he conceded. "Okay, we'll skip the chitchat and get right to business." Glancing down at his desk, he began shuffling through paper.

Jolene looked him over as he worked. Today he had a challenging tilt to his chin and a rakish twinkle in his eyes, a tiny spark of impudent arrogance that was intriguing rather than annoying. He had all the confidence in the world around the female gender. It was obvious that most women found him utterly irresistible. But a sense of resolve made her raise an eyebrow. It was a good thing she wasn't like most women.

Once he'd found the paper he was searching for, he sat back and looked at her, enjoying what he saw. Yes, she would be the perfect girl for Tony.

"I won't keep you long," he told her, tapping his pencil on the paper. "I just have a few questions."

She crossed her legs and nodded. "Did you want me to fill out tax forms or…?"

He waved that away. "No, we won't bother with that stuff yet. I just want to go over some questions with you."

She nodded, perfectly willing. "All right."

"Personal information," he added, glancing at her and then down at the paper he had before him on the desk.

Something in his voice put her on notice. "What?"

Ignoring her question, he stared hard at the paper and began. "Uh, let's see. Are you married?"

She frowned, uneasy and not sure why. "I think you know the answer to that one. My friend Mandy said you'd asked her."

He looked up. "Mandy runs the pretzel machine?"

She nodded, her silvery eyes watching him steadily.

He smiled quickly and picked up his pen, jotting down a mark. "Okay. We'll move on, then. Is the little boy—Kevin is his name, isn't it? Is he your only child?"

She nodded again, and he made another mark on the paper.

"Are you seeing anyone special right now?"

Her frowned deepened and her suspicions grew. "What does that have to do with how well I can handle marzipan?" she asked him.

His smile was suave and reassuring. "Nothing. Nothing at all. These are just questions on a psychological profile. They mean nothing."

She smelled a rat, but she had to admit, his smile was persuasive and she found herself on the verge of smiling back. "Then why bother with them?" she murmured.

He shrugged disarmingly. "Like I say, it's a profile. We like to know what kind of people our employees are." He tapped the desk with the pencil. "You didn't answer the question. Are you seeing anyone special?" And his gaze held hers as though he would read more in her silver eyes than she would tell him with her lips.

Slowly, reluctantly, she shook her head.

He noted her reply on the paper and moved on, but his eyes were alight with satisfaction. "Okay. Now—would you say you're the kind of woman who, uh, works best with a lot of people around, with light support and supervision, or on her own?''

She hesitated. This actually sounded like it might be a legitimate question for a profile. "I'd say probably somewhere between the last two," she said, and he nodded.

"Would you say you're the kind of woman who likes walks on a moonlight beach, a good game of tennis, or dancing the night away at nightclubs."

They were swerving into suspicious territory again, but there was something about the sneaky way he was doing it that made her want to laugh.

"I'm the kind of woman who likes to stay home and play with my son," she told him candidly. "And that's about it."

"Okay." He nodded. "Then how about this. Do you go for men of action, or the strong, silent type?"

Now she knew it was a hoax. How did he even have the nerve? "What?" she said, on the verge of laughter.

He spoke quickly as though he wanted to get his question in before she got up and walked out on him. "Okay, make it multiple choice. Would you prefer a man of action, the strong silent type, a sensitive poet, or the caring, compassionate and deeply loving, father of an eleven-year-old girl?"

She was shaking her head, holding back her laugh.

"Who happens to be very handsome and even funny, when you get him in the right mood," he added, humor gleaming in his dark eyes.

The jig was up. She knew he wasn't serious. He was going to ask her out, wasn't he? And yet, she couldn't help but be a little flattered by it. After all, he was a very attractive man. Still, she was going to have to set him straight.

"Now you sound like something on the dating game," she told him, trying to be stern. "Bachelor number one or bachelor number two?" She threw up her hands. "Who cares? I'll pick none of the above, thank you." Her gaze met his calmly. "The truth is, I don't date."

Somehow he didn't look convinced. "Never?"

She shook her head. "No, never."

He leaned forward on the desk and gazed at her earnestly. "But what if you met that great guy with the daughter and you hit it off right away and—"

She frowned and broke into his question. "Listen, am I here for a job or is this all a ploy just to get a date?"

"A date?" He had the gall to look puzzled by her reaction. "Oh, wait. You think I…"

Yes, she did, and she'd decided it was time to put an end to this. Rising, she reached for her bag. "I'm sorry, but I won't go out with you. And I would advise you to find a new pickup line. This one really stinks."

He was laughing at her. She could see it in his eyes, but she couldn't for the life of her see why he would find this amusing.

"I think there must have been a misunderstanding…" he began.

She sighed. It looked as if she was going to have to be explicit. "That's just the point," she told him sweetly. "You see, I never planned to go out with you. That's not why I came."

He blinked. "Well, that's good," he said, his voice almost too hearty. "Because I never planned to ask you."

"Oh, come on," she began, but a small hint of unease began to tickle deep inside. After all, nothing up to this point had made much sense, had it?

"Seriously, I didn't bring you in here to ask you out on a date."

"And he'd better not," said a chirpy voice from behind her. "Because that would mean that he would have to stand me up. And I get ugly when I get stood up."

Jolene hadn't noticed the door opening, but she whirled to behold a pretty young woman with long black hair and bangs that barely cleared her huge blue eyes leaning in the doorway. Grant rose, coughing delicately into his hand in a way that Jolene later realized could only have been to hide his grin.

"Uh, Jolene Campbell, this is Kim Mancini—my date for this evening."

"Your..."

"Yes. As a matter of fact, Kim and I have been dating for about three months now. Isn't that right, sweetheart?"

"Uh-huh." Kim nodded her head perkily. "We met at my cousin's wedding. I fell in the swimming pool and Grant pulled me out by my hair." She giggled. "Isn't that romantic?"

"Very," Jolene agreed with a weak smile.

Grant rose from behind his desk and came around quickly, as though to get between the two women before things got messy. "Well, I guess we'll see you bright and early tomorrow morning," he said, shaking Jolene's hand and smiling in a way that said clearly the interview was over. "How would eight do? I'm glad you've decided to join us."

Jolene managed to salvage a smile before she turned to go. When she glanced back as she closed the door, she saw Kim melting into Grant's arms, and the blush that had begun creeping up her neck a few minutes earlier made a major surge up and over her cheeks. She took a very deep breath and made her escape to the parking lot.

Humiliation? That was too wimpy a word for what she was feeling. She fell into the driver's seat of her car and let out a silent scream before starting the engine. If only there was a way to rewind life and do it over.

Four

"**Y**ou can imagine what a fool I felt like," Jolene sighed as she talked to Mandy later that evening, as the two of them shared hot cocoa on the couch. Kevin was in his bed, sound asleep, the two women were both in pajamas, talking softly in the dim lamplight.

"In fact, the only time in my life when I've felt more of a fool," Jolene went on, "was one time in church when I gave a blistering lecture to some young guy who winked at me. I'd just been named May Queen at school and I was feeling pretty full of myself, I guess. Anyway, this poor sap sat there while I lectured, turning red, and finally managed to mumble to me that he was actually winking at his fiancée who was sitting in the pew behind me."

Mandy laughed, propping her feet in their panda slippers up on the coffee table. "Not good."

"No." Jolene shook her head, remembering. "Half the congregation heard the whole thing and there was definitely some snickering in the ranks." She sighed sadly, her silver eyes full of tragedy. "But in many ways, this was worse. I can't tell you exactly why. It just was." She groaned and threw back her head. "Do I have to go back there tomorrow? Isn't there some way I could win the lottery or find out some rich uncle left me all his fortune so I don't have to go?"

Mandy popped a marshmallow into her mouth and shook her head. "The lottery isn't until Saturday and you told me you didn't have any living relatives."

"That's just the point, silly," Jolene muttered, grabbing her cocoa mug and holding it to her as if it were a life preserver. "He wouldn't have to be living, would he? Hah. Got you there."

Mandy laughed, but quickly sobered, looking at her friend guiltily. "Well, if you really can't stand the thought of going back there, I could always..."

Jolene picked up a pillow and threatened her with it. "If you say one more word about going back to that horrible factory job, I'll bean you with this. I'm a big girl, Mandy." Dropping the pillow, she lifted her chin in mock heroic fashion. "I can handle humiliation and ridicule. I can handle having Grant think I'm an addle-pated ego maniac. I'm tough and I'm desperate—always a strong combination."

Mandy stared at her friend for a long moment, then gave a slight shrug. "Jolene, what about contacting Jeff? You know where he is now, and he is Kevin's father. He ought to provide some support..."

"No." Jolene said it abruptly, with a tone of finality that should have put an end to the discussion. But seeing the look on Mandy's face, she relented and tried to explain.

"As far as I'm concerned, Jeff was no more a father to Kevin than...than the milkman could have been. Just handing over some genes doesn't make a father out of a man.

Loving and caring and attention are what do it. And that Kevin never got from Jeff."

Mandy raised a knowing eyebrow. "Legally he owes you."

Jolene nodded. "But practically, we're better off without him."

There it was, short and sweet. She could see that Mandy didn't agree, but Mandy didn't have a child and an ex-husband who had run out on her. Rising, she carried both their mugs out to the kitchen to rinse them, as though the activity would take up her mind and keep out the memories. But it didn't work. They came anyway.

Short and sweet. That was her entire life. Well, maybe short and not so sweet was more like it. She'd met Jeff in junior college. She was majoring in culinary arts and nutrition and he was majoring in partying 101. Actually he was a drama major, bound for the silver screen someday, or so he said. She should have known better. She *did* know better. She'd grown up in a working-class family and she knew you had to struggle for the good things in life, that luxuries didn't fall into your lap just because you wanted them to, that being an actor was pretty pie in the sky, that guys who could act had probably done a lot of practicing at lying. But his dazzling smile, his gorgeous tan, his china blue eyes, all had blinded her and she'd married him.

To this day she couldn't believe she'd done it. It had all happened so fast. He'd wanted to get intimate and she'd said not without a wedding ring and he'd said, okay, as easy as that and they'd raced off to Las Vegas before she could catch her breath.

"There you go," she thought to herself now. *Marry in haste, repent at leisure,* her grandma had always said. Grandma was great for advice. She'd also warned Jolene never to marry a man who wore a thick gold chain around his neck. "You can see right away that he's vain as a peacock," she'd said.

"And Grandma was never wrong," Jolene murmured. Vain as a peacock. That pretty well described Jeff. One good thing was she'd learned her lesson. She would never fall for a pretty boy again.

Jeff was long gone now. All it had taken was the news that Kevin was on the way and he'd already had his bag half packed.

"Don't you see, Jolene," he told her earnestly, as though he just couldn't understand why she didn't want the best for him just like he did. "If I'm ever going to make it in Hollywood I have to be free to focus all my psychic energy on the goal. If I get distracted by other things, I might lose the race. I can't afford to let that happen."

Inevitably, they'd divorced. She'd heard he was up in Alaska doing theater-in-the-round in dinner houses. What that was doing to his psychic energy she could only guess. But she hadn't seen him since the day he'd left and after all this time, she'd given up hoping he would ever want to have any sort of relationship with Kevin. It was not to be, and by now, she was glad. She had Kevin all to herself and that was the way they liked it.

But Mandy was right about one thing—they did need more money. Much as it embarrassed her to go back and face Grant, that was exactly what she was going to do. Hopefully some good would come of it. Taking in a deep breath, she crossed her fingers for luck.

Jolene walked into the restaurant hiding her unease with a quick, confident step, a bright smile, and Kevin settled jauntily in her arms. She glanced around for Grant, but he was nowhere to be seen. Maybe it was too early for him, she reasoned, feeling a sense of relief that she could put off seeing him.

Michelle was there, looking crisp and efficient and beautifully dressed in a pale teal cashmere suit. She greeted Jolene warmly, introducing her to two maintenance workers, then helping her set up the playpen in the break room. Kevin would be staying in a room right off the kitchen and accessible through an open door.

"I hope this is going to work out," Jolene said as she realized how thoroughly her attention was going to be divided between her son and her baking. Looking at the top of his downy head, she felt her heart lurch. Was she going to be able to do this?

"Of course it will," Michelle told her reassuringly, patting her arm. "We'll all help out watching him. After all, most days you'll be finished with your work by the time the lunch crowd comes in. We'll manage."

Jolene turned to look at the woman, a little surprised and intrigued. Why would Michelle go out of her way to make this possible? She couldn't imagine, and was just about to thank her for it, when Grant's voice came into the room and she froze, her smile pasted on her face.

Here it was. She was going to have to face him and read his thoughts in his eyes. Would he be thinking about what had happened the afternoon before? How could either one of them avoid it?

Here goes, she thought to herself as she turned. *The best defense is a good offense.* And she gave him her brightest smile. "Good morning," she chirped. "Should we go over menus before I get started?"

Grant looked at her, bemused by her aggressive cheerfulness, but glad she didn't show any signs of planning to hold the misunderstanding of the day before against him. He knew she'd been embarrassed, knew it was mostly his

fault that she'd fallen into that trap. But he also knew in-
stinctively that to apologize for it now would be the worst
thing he could have done. He'd learned most of what he
knew about women from Stephanie, his ex-wife. If this had
happened to her, he knew very well how she would have
made him pay for having embarrassed her.

But Jolene was different. He liked the way she looked,
liked the stonewashed jeans that hugged her legs and bottom, the soft baby blue sweater that seemed to drape around
her breasts in a way that would set any male pulse pounding. The more he was getting to know her, the more he
was beginning to realize that she was special. And that was
just what he wanted to find for Tony, a woman way above
the ordinary. Tony deserved the best, and if Jolene turned
out to be as exceptional as she seemed, he was going to
make sure the two of them got together.

The only thing that bothered him was the way he was
reacting to her. Those silver eyes seemed to cut right
through him and something in them spurred his pulse rate
just a little higher.

It's all metaphysical, he told himself silently. *Ignore it.
The tingling will go away. She's meant for Tony, and that's
the way it's going to be.*

He gazed at her for a long moment before he answered,
and Jolene could have sworn there was a look of relief in
his eyes. What had he been worried about, that she might
throw herself at him bodily? Was he thinking, *Oh, good, it
looks as though she's going to act normally today?* It was
only by an act of supreme will that she kept from blushing
again.

"I'm glad you came," he said at last. "I have a feeling
we're going to make dessert history together."

"What in the world makes you think that?" she asked

him, but she couldn't help but respond to his knowing smile.

"Vibes," he told her. "Can't you feel it? This is going to be classic. I'm the king and you're Michelangelo. I'm the archduke and you're Mozart."

She laughed. "If you're saying that you are the money-bags and I'm the talent," she protested, "I think you'd better lower your expectations a little. I'm going for good food here, not classic art."

"Go for great food and we'll compromise," he said, smiling at her, his dark eyes just a little too intimate for comfort.

She tried to look stern and professional. "The menus?" she prompted.

"Sure," he said, putting out an arm to help steer her his way. "Come on into my office and…"

She resisted. "I'd rather stay out here where I can keep an eye on Kevin," she reminded him quickly, and he turned, frowning as he sighted the playpen in the next room through the open door.

"Ah, yes, Kevin," he said dryly, and there was an obvious lack of enthusiasm in his tone.

The child caught sight of him at the same time and his face lit up. "Cookie!" he cried, pointing at the man and bouncing with obvious delight. "Cookie, cookie, cookie!"

Everyone in the kitchen laughed and Grant even managed a wan smile. "Hello, Kevin," he said, nodding at the child. "Sorry, no cookies today."

Turning, he looked balefully at his staff. "Don't you people have anything better to do?" he asked them, but Jolene thought she saw a twinkle in his eyes. She certainly hoped so. If he and Kevin got off on the wrong foot, her pastry chef career probably wouldn't last long.

"Have you met everyone?" he was asking as he ushered

her back to the table in the corner of the room, and she looked around quickly, smiling at the few who had the time to look up.

"This is Picard, our chef," Grant said, nodding to a tall, muscular man with a wide grin who gave her an appraising look that was as flattering as a silent wolf whistle before leaning forward to shake her hand.

"The name's Gus Blount," he advised her heartily. "The Picard thing is just for the customers. I don't know why they think they have to have French guys cooking their food, but they seem to like it."

She couldn't help but laugh. He was handsome in a rough way and his accent sounded closer to the Bronx than to *Paree,* yet he had a comical way of expressing himself. "But, can't they tell right away when they talk to you?" she asked him.

He shook his head, his eyes sparkling. "I never say a word. I just smile and shake my head, as though I don't really understand English, and they give up after a while." He demonstrated his silent look and she laughed again.

"Do you know any French at all?" she asked him, lingering though she knew Grant was waiting.

He shrugged. "Not a word. But what the heck, a smile is the same in all languages."

"That it is," she said, touched for a moment by the truth in his words and the evidence of a streak of poetry in his soul.

He gave her a cheery wave and went back to measuring ingredients for some dish he was working on and Jolene turned back, warmed by the reception she was getting. Everyone she had met so far was friendly and welcoming. Grant was the only one who put her on edge.

Just as she'd thought, he was waiting for her. When she turned to find him, he had his arms crossed and was leaning against the corner desk with the look of a man who was about to start tapping his foot. She had a quick moment to take him in, note his cool dark eyes, the straight, even eyebrows, the full lips that gave a sense of toughness one moment, a sense of tenderness the next.

"Sorry," she told him as she hurried to his side. "I didn't mean to keep you waiting." But she met his gaze with a slightly defiant spark in her silver eyes, a spark that belied her words.

And to her surprise, his wide mouth curved with amusement and the next thing she knew, he was laughing at her again. "Don't mention it," he told her. "I've got infinite patience."

She frowned, not sure that wasn't meant as a dig somehow, but before she could retort, someone new came into the kitchen and she found Grant looking behind her and gesturing for a plump middle-aged woman to come forward to be introduced as well.

"This is Fou Fou," he told Jolene as he had them both shake hands. "She'll be your assistant."

"I...I'm going to have an assistant?" Jolene stammered out. Such a thing had never occurred to her.

"Sure," he told her airily. "But don't let it go to your head. Fou Fou assists anyone who needs her. She's our resident gofer. Aren't you, Fou Fou?"

The woman's badly bleached hair bobbed vigorously and she said something incomprehensible that might have been French. On the other hand, it might have been Norwegian. Jolene wasn't sure she would have known the difference, not when it was spoken so quickly and was so completely incomprehensible.

"Fou Fou?" Jolene asked her, still somewhat bewildered. "Your name is Fou Fou?"

"*Oui, oui.*" Her makeup looked as though it had been

put on with a trowel, but she smiled with evident goodwill and shook Jolene's hand again with cheerful energy. "Fou Fou."

The language and accent were, by now, unmistakable. "You must be French," Jolene said firmly, but she looked to Grant for confirmation.

He shook his head. "She's not French," he explained patiently. "She's from Switzerland."

"Okay," Jolene said agreeably. "But she speaks French."

"Mais oui," Fou Fou responded in her childlike voice with its heavy accent. "Also Italian. And *un poco de español.*"

Jolene smiled at her. "That ought to come in very handy with those darn old Spanish tart recipes," she joked, but no one else seemed to catch on to pastry humor, and she killed the smile and glanced at Grant as Fou Fou bowed and backed away.

"She certainly looks French," she noted softly to her new boss as they both watched the woman leave the room.

"True. Like something out of a Toulouse-Lautrec painting." He sighed pointedly and raised an eyebrow. "I'm not sure that's the image we're going for here, but beggars can't be choosers where the French are concerned."

"You mean...?"

"I mean there just aren't enough French chefs and French maids and French waitresses to go around these days. We make do with what we can get."

Jolene's eyes narrowed. "Ah. Please don't say you want me to dress in a little black uniform with a lacy French cap."

He grinned, enchanted by the thought. "What a great idea. I'll look into it right away."

She opened her mouth to protest, but quickly decided he

must be joking. It might be best if she moved on. She shut her mouth again and smiled. He had menus with him, and she was anxious to see what he had in mind for her today.

They went over menus for the next fifteen minutes. She took notes on a little spiral notepad she kept with her, and every few minutes she glanced over at the break room to make sure Kevin was still playing happily with his toys and not bothering anyone. It was going to be hard keeping an eye on him while she had her mind on her work. It was going to take practice and she was going to have to be vigilant, starting right away. She would try. But she wasn't looking when he launched his attack on Grant.

The first she knew of it was when Grant cried out and grabbed his ankle.

"Hey!" he said, glaring at her crossly. "Your kid threw a block at me."

Protective mother that she was, she went into immediate denial. "No, he didn't."

"Then what's this?" Grant asked, picking up a toy off the floor.

"Oh, that's his all right," she said quickly. "But he didn't throw it *at* you. He…he merely threw it, and it hit you." She could see he didn't believe it and she added quickly, "He's a baby. He can't aim." And at the same time, she threw a suspicious sideways glance at her son. He was grinning ear to ear.

"Oh, yeah?" Grant was not going to let this go, though his grumble was muted and he was obviously feeling a little silly about the whole thing. "I saw him. He had a glint in his eye and then he hauled off and aimed right at me." He rubbed his sore shin, but he managed a wobbly grin. "You know, the kid's got an arm. Keep an eye on him. He may be worth big bucks in the major leagues some day."

"Cookie!" Kevin called, and Grant made a face.

"Of course, he will have to broaden his vocabulary just a bit," he murmured, turning back to the menus.

Jolene hid her smile and tried to look serious. She was awfully lucky she'd found a job where she could have Kevin with her. Now if she could just keep her son from alienating the boss, everything would be just fine.

The tables were set and ready for the dinner crowd and cakes and pastries filled the counters in the kitchen. Grant came out onto the floor and slid into the booth across from where his hostess was folding napkins.

"Well, Michelle," he asked her, leaning forward and talking quietly. "What do you think?"

Michelle looked at him for a moment, noted the eagerness in his eyes, then laughed softly, shaking her head. "I think you've got a long row to hoe, my boy," she told him with gentle affection mixed with doubt.

He frowned. "Why? She seems like a great girl, doesn't she?"

Michelle nodded as she smoothed out another napkin. "So she seems." She hesitated, then added, "She has eyes like a husky."

"A husky." He grinned. "I like that. Her eyes are spectacular, aren't they? She's very special. But that's what Tony deserves."

"Maybe. But you ought to give it a bit more time. You don't know her well enough yet to make a final judgment on that."

"I think I know her well enough to say she'd make a perfect match for Tony."

Michelle seemed to swallow hard before meeting his gaze again, and when she did, she reached out and patted his cheek with her long, slender fingers. "Take it easy, Grant. I'm not sure she's his type," she murmured.

Grant wasn't one to let a little cynicism rain on his parade, but he'd counted on Michelle's support and she just wasn't giving it as easily as he would have liked.

"At this point, Tony doesn't have a type," he grumbled. "His type is a box of popcorn on a Saturday night while he watches the late movie on TV." He grimaced and flexed his wide shoulders with impatience. "Michelle, don't you see? We've got to get him out of his rut."

The use of the plural pronoun made her grimace, but she didn't protest. Instead she looked down at her hands. "Maybe he likes his rut," she suggested softly.

He shook his head, certain of his point of view and oblivious to any other. "No, we're going to change his life for him. It's way past time to do it."

She raised an arched eyebrow and gazed at him levelly. "You have a plan, I presume?"

"Sure, I've got a thousand of them. If one doesn't work, we move on to the next. One way or another..."

"He's not going to like this," she noted, frowning as she began to realize Grant was bound and determined to see this thing through and no amount of pessimism was going to deter him.

Grant nodded, a smile beginning to turn up the corners of his wide mouth. He had a feeling she was softening. "That's why we have to be crafty about it. And that's where you come in."

She looked startled. "Me?"

"Sure." He gave her a glimpse of the smile that charmed most women he came in contact with. "Everyone knows females are sneakier than men. That's the main reason I want you in on this deal."

She didn't bother to react to the sexist statement. She had deeper problems with what he'd said. "You want my help in getting Tony together with a bright young woman you only met three days ago.'' She glanced at him to see if he'd detected the bitter note she'd tried to hide but was afraid had probably shown through.

But he didn't notice at all. He was intent on his project and nothing was going to hold him back. He heard her statement and nodded, his dark eyes clear and bright. ''What's wrong with that?''

Michelle stared at him for a long moment, then shook her head. "I don't know. There's something about it." She stopped herself and decided on the truth. "I...I really don't like it, Grant.''

He narrowed his eyes as though she were speaking a language he couldn't quite understand. Shaking his head as though to push her words away, he continued, ''Michelle, I've got to do this. You know how much I owe Tony.''

Michelle recoiled. "Grant, you don't owe Tony anything.''

But he nodded. "Yes, I do. I owe him everything. Listen, here's the plan. It's basic. It's simple.'' He looked into her eyes to make sure she was with him, or at least listening. ''I'm going to work on Jolene. You're going to work on Tony. It'll be up to you to make him see how important it is for him to give this a chance.''

Michelle stared at him openmouthed for a moment, then let out a gurgle of laughter. ''Dream on, my friend.''

''Come on,'' he coaxed. ''How long has it been since you two have gotten together? You're old friends. It would be no big deal for you to call him up and go over to see him.''

She stood, taking her pile of folded napkins up in her arms in preparation for carrying them away with her. ''Do your own dirty work,'' she told him serenely. ''If you want to marry your brother off to Miss Bright Eyes, you are going to have to do it on your own. I'm not helping you.''

"What's the matter?" he asked, frowning up at her as though he could hardly believe what he was hearing. "Don't you like her?"

Michelle opened her mouth to answer, but before she could, a voice interrupted.

"Excuse me."

They both swung around to find Jolene smiling at them tranquilly, her baby in her arms.

"I'm finished in the kitchen. Unless someone chokes on my pie crust or gets ptomaine from my lemon meringue, I guess I'll see you tomorrow."

Michelle managed a wan smile but Grant rose and nodded to her. "Uh, thanks for coming, Jolene. I...I'm sure the things you've prepared are going to be fine. See you in the morning," he added as she started toward the door with a cheery wave. He watched her go, then turned back to frown at Michelle.

"How much do you think she heard?" he asked her gruffly.

Michelle shook her head. "I can't tell. Were we being that explicit?"

He flashed her a baleful look. "We could have done without the 'Miss Bright Eyes' comment."

Michelle caught her lip between her teeth to keep from laughing.

He shrugged. "Never mind," he said grimly. "My mind is made up. She's going to marry my brother if I have to trick them both into it."

Michelle sighed as he strode toward the kitchen. She knew Grant and she knew Tony and she was very much afraid disaster was looming on the horizon.

"Oh, well," she murmured to herself. "There hasn't been a good fight in the Fargo family since their father died. Maybe it's time for one."

Five

Two days went by before Grant was able to get Tony to come into the restaurant so that he could attempt to set his plan in motion. In those two days, Jolene made thirty-two Napoleons and twenty-four éclairs, six apple pies and sixteen fudge cakes, already given the name The Chocolate Revenge by the waiters, along with various and sundry other delicious concoctions. There was general agreement around the Grill—Grant had found a treasure in Jolene.

Meanwhile, Fou Fou burned every bakery item she came in contact with and had to be confined to mixing batches and greasing pans. Picard had taken to serenading the kitchen with his surprisingly good tenor voice, enchanting Jolene and annoying Grant. The irrepressible Kevin had thrown another block, a plastic ring and two animal crackers at Grant, not all at the same time, and also called him "Cookie!" whenever he came into view, a gesture of goodwill that somehow failed to endear him to the boss.

But Grant gritted his teeth and bore up under the general hilarity Kevin caused, because without Kevin, he wouldn't have Jolene, and the more he knew of Jolene, the more he was sure she was exactly the right woman for his brother.

And Jolene had been given the full graduate course on what a great guy Tony was every time Grant got a chance to get a statement in edgewise. She heard all about his kindness to strangers, his superiority at crossword puzzles, his devotion to his daughter, and above everything, his loyalty to his mother.

This lesson in the wonders of Tony often happened when Jolene was up to her elbows in flour and powdered sugar and had no means of escape. Grant would lean against the counter as though he were supervising and somehow the conversation would come around to the same old topic every time.

"My brother, Tony…did I ever tell you about my brother, Tony? I did? I wasn't sure. Anyway, the first thing Tony did when he got his first job was to buy our mother a kitten. She always wanted a kitten and my father always had to have dogs. We had boxers and German shepherds and setters, but she just kept pining for a kitten. So Tony took his very first paycheck and bought Mama a fluffy little Persian and—"

"Excuse me, Grant," Jolene broke in carefully. "But did you say you wanted lemon custard or cream whip in these shells?"

"Uh, lemon, I think." Grant glanced down at the ingredients she was assembling on the counter and nodded. "Yeah, lemon. Anyway, Tony got Mama this kitten and it was the cutest little thing. She carried it around like a baby and…Michelle, tell Jolene about the kitten Tony bought for Mama."

Michelle, who had just entered the room and hadn't expected to be corralled into helping him with his campaign, shot him a look that had daggers coming out of it. "The kitten must have been after my time. As I remember it, your mama was allergic to cat hair."

Grant frowned. "But Tony..."

"Tony probably forgot," Michelle said evenly, though she smiled sweetly at Jolene. "Why is it that men always forget these little things?" She glanced at Grant and made a face behind Jolene's back. "Watch out or I'll tell everyone about the time Tony tied you up in the tree house and your parents searched the neighborhood for two hours before he finally confessed and told them where you were."

Grant's handsome face registered horror. "Michelle!"

Michelle smiled smugly. "Tony was an arrogant little monster in his time," she told Jolene, ignoring Grant's sputtering. "When you come right down to it, Grant was the nicer of the two. He was certainly the one you could count on when it came to sticking up for you on the playground when the bullies came to call."

"Tony stood up for me all the time," Grant protested, frowning at her furiously, and the two of them moved toward the doorway, still arguing.

Jolene smiled, listening to them. She had no idea why Grant was always telling her about his brother, but she found it endearing. He displayed a family feeling that she approved of.

She liked families, big or small. She liked the idea of families, the dream, the ideal of Christmas with green-and-red decorations and presents under the tree and Thanksgiving with people crowded around the carving of the turkey and Easter with children dashing around carrying colorful baskets and hunting for eggs. She liked family dinners and families that sang together and family night at the roller rink.

It wasn't that she'd never had a family of her own. She'd grown up in one. At least, it could be called a family. Her brother was fifteen years older than she was and he was out of the house before she really knew him. Her mother worked as a seamstress for one of the movie studios and seemed to prefer ten-hour days, while her father was a bus driver for the Metropolitan system and an avid bowler who belonged to three or four leagues at a time and was seldom home himself. So Jolene's family had existed mostly in her imagination. They never did the things families were supposed to do together. But she could dream about them, try to reach for them.

It always seemed as though she were in too much of a hurry trying to catch up to other people, trying to catch up to where they were, and by the time she got there, they'd moved on. It had only been since Kevin was born that she'd begun to relax a little. The only way she was going to have a family, the only way Kevin was going to have a family, was if Jolene made one for them. That was going to take time, effort, energy. She knew it didn't just happen because you wanted it to. It would take planning, thinking, paying attention. And at the same time, there was a living that had to be made.

She looked around the kitchen, looked at Picard singing over his roux and Fou Fou humming along as she measured out flour and she felt a smile bubbling from deep inside her. This just might turn out to be the best job she'd ever had. Everyone had been so nice and Grant...well, he was turning out to be a boss unlike any she'd ever worked for. In fact, she didn't mind him so much anymore. If the truth be known, she sort of liked him.

Just as she finished sifting out flour, Kevin made himself known. He was fussy today and she supposed he must be teething or something. Still in her happy glow, she dusted off her hands and went in to see to him. Having him near was part of what made this all so perfect. For now.

Grant led Michelle from the kitchen so he could talk to her away from Jolene. They ended up leaning against the fake railing in the middle of the room—the decorative piece that was supposed to keep children from climbing on the reconstructed Apache campsite that sat in the place of honor in the center of everything. The waiters and waitresses cursed it daily because it was right in the flow of traffic, but customers liked it. And it was a natural gathering place.

"I'm just trying to butter her up where Tony is concerned," Grant tried to explain to Michelle. "You're undercutting my efforts."

Michelle rolled her eyes heavenward. "Your efforts are ridiculous. I haven't seen a more transparent sales job since that French guy with the big nose hid in the bushes and fed romantic lines to whoever the other guy was trying to woo the lady."

"His name was Cyrano," Grant said gruffly. "And this is completely different."

Michelle raised a questioning eyebrow. "Oh yeah? How?"

Grant stared at her, perplexed by her obstructionism. Surely she could see the contrast here. "I'm not in love with her myself," he explained patiently. "My whole purpose is to match her up with Tony."

Michelle made a rude noise.

Grant frowned, then decided Michelle was teasing him and shook his head. "This is important, Michelle. It's hard to find a nice girl for someone like Tony. I mean, he's got an eleven-year-old daughter and all…"

His manner was so earnest, Michelle relented a bit, but

she still couldn't resist asking him, "Why don't you just give him one of your old girlfriends? You've got a ton of them. How about that Kim Mancini? Didn't you just dump her?"

"That's not the kind of girl Tony needs and you know it." Grant leaned back and a superior look came over his handsome face. "When you get older, you begin to realize that you're not just marrying a playmate to share the rest of your days with. You're also marrying the mother of your children." He glanced at her. "Scary thought, isn't it?"

She snorted again. "Only if you're dating girls like Kim," she noted dryly.

Before he could answer, or even strangle her—an impulse that did come to mind—the main door opened and let in a crack of sunlight and then a long, tall body in white slacks and a royal blue Hawaiian shirt that could only be...

"Tony!" Grant cried out, striding forward to greet his brother. "You came!"

"Hi." Tony returned the quick hug and looked around the restaurant, which he hadn't been in for quite a while. "Listen, I got the message on my machine and I came right over, but I'm in sort of a hurry. Allison is at her Girl Scout meeting but I'm supposed to pick her up in fifteen minutes, so if you'll just let me in on what the big emergency is...." He looked at his brother questioningly.

Grant hesitated. "Hey, you got here really quickly," he said enthusiastically, playing for time. "I thought you'd call first."

"Why?" His brother looked at him curiously. "What's up?"

"Uh..." His gaze shifted. Now that Tony was here, he wasn't ready. He hadn't really thought up much of a good lie yet. Michelle stepped into the circle of brightness from the skylight and he looked at her with relief. "Say, Tony, look who's here. I bet you two haven't seen each other in a long time, have you?''

Tony turned, did a genuine double take and made a long, low whistle under his breath. "Michelle," he said, shaking his head. "It's been so long. You...you really look good."

Michelle was smiling up into his face. "You, too," she said softly.

Grant made an impatient sound. He wanted to get on with things, but he managed to rein in his impulses and pretend to be polite. "Well, it's been a while for you two, huh?" he said, looking at them. "I remember when the two of you—" he began.

Michelle flashed him a warning look and broke in. "Don't look back," she advised quickly. "Something may be gaining on you."

Tony grinned. "Who said that?" he asked.

Michelle shrugged. "Some deep philosopher."

Grant frowned and shook his head. "No, I think it was a baseball player," he said, but they weren't paying any attention to him.

"Michelle," Tony was saying again, looking her up and down. "You just look so good."

Grant grabbed his arm to keep him from getting bogged down. "Yeah, yeah, we all know how Michelle looks." *It's the new pastry chef I want you to take a look at,* he was thinking, but aloud, he said, "We have no time to reminisce over the old days. You just said you have to pick up Allison any minute. So...uh...look, I'd like you to come into the kitchen with me. I want your advice on something."

Michelle was shaking her head and he frowned at her, annoyed at the distraction. "What?" he asked shortly.

"Tell him the truth," Michelle said, looking at Tony from under her long auburn lashes.

Grant made a gesture of exasperation, then leaned close and whispered near her ear. "But you said we'd have to lie to him to get him to do this," he reminded her.

She shook her head again, her gaze on his brother. "I never said that. I said that telling him would ruin everything."

"Exactly my point."

"But I've changed my mind. Tell him the truth. He's your brother, and he deserves that much."

Grant turned, scowling. It was too late to do anything else now. Michelle had poisoned the well. Tony was looking very perplexed.

"What's going on?" he asked, looking from one of them to the other.

Grant put his hands into his pockets and grimaced. "Okay, here's the deal. I hired a pastry chef."

Tony shook his head with a half grin. "Congratulations. I approve." He made a gesture toward the front door. "Can I go now?"

Grant moved closer and looked into his face. "That's not it. There's more. This new pastry chef...she's a woman." He watched his brother for his reaction. "A very nice and pretty woman," he added with extra significance.

Tony's eyes narrowed and he groaned. "I'm beginning to get a bad feeling about this," he muttered.

Grant was shaking his head, his eyes bright. "Tony, listen. You're really going to like her. She's...she's perfect for you."

Tony threw up his hands and turned toward the door. "That's it. I'm out of here."

"No, wait," Grant insisted, grabbing his arm and trying to turn him toward the kitchen. "You've got to meet her. She's..."

Tony looked at his brother with exasperation. "I don't

care if you've hired Sharon Stone to make your pies and cakes. I'm not interested.''

"Tony, come on, be reasonable. You need to get out and..."

Tony wasn't listening. He was heading for the door and Grant threw Michelle a desperate look. Rising from where she'd been leaning, Michelle set her own tall frame in motion, reaching the exit before Tony did.

She put out one hand, which landed on his chest and stopped him cold. "Think again, Tony," she told him calmly. "You know what Grant is like when he gets an idea he won't shake. He'll drive us all nuts. Get it over with. Go meet the woman or he'll be after you every day until you do.''

Tony hesitated, staring down into her sultry eyes. "What am I supposed to do, just walk in and say, 'Hi, I came in to look you over'?''

"No problem," Grant said, relief evident in his voice. "Come on. Just come into the kitchen with me and I'll..."

Tony glared at him. "I didn't say I'd do it.''

Michelle smiled at him. "But you will," she announced.

He gave her a long, slow grin. "Michelle, you always did have a way of making me do what you wanted." He sighed. "Okay. Let's get it over with.''

Grant nodded and started toward the kitchen, but Tony stopped him.

"No. I'll go alone. I refuse to go in there like a small parade. It's just too obvious.'' He shrugged, looking from Grant to Michelle and back. "I'll say I'm looking for you," he decided.

"Good idea," Grant said quickly. Anything as long as he saw Jolene. He was firmly convinced that seeing her was all it would take. "Go on. We'll just wait out here.''

They both watched as Tony left for the kitchen, his long-legged, slightly disjointed-looking stride so familiar to both of them. Then they turned and looked at each other.

"Thanks," Grant said briefly, sighing deeply. "I was afraid for a minute there that I would have to hog-tie him."

She didn't answer, her face bemused. "He looks older," she noted, "but not old."

Grant chuckled. "He looks like the same old Tony, only melted a little."

Michelle made a face at that one, but Grant didn't notice. His mind was consumed with what was going on in the kitchen. "He's looking at her right now," he mused. "What do you want to bet it'll be love at first sight?"

Michelle turned as though she'd suddenly remembered she must surely have something better to do. "I'd bet the house against it," she told him crisply. "Intelligent men in their thirties don't fall in love at first sight. That's only for the young and stupid."

Grant was shaking his head in complete disagreement. "I mean, I don't know this from firsthand experience," he admitted. "I'm not the type. But I do know some people fall in love that way, head over heels, like walking into a tiger trap. And that can be a beautiful thing. Remember when Tony met Mary...?"

Michelle was saved from having to remember that because a door slammed and they both spun toward the kitchen, startled. Tony was hurrying back through the room. He swung in front of his brother and looked him up and down.

"What was that, Grant, some kind of joke?" he muttered, obviously trying not to be loud enough to be overheard back at the kitchen, despite his annoyance.

Grant didn't get it. "What?" he asked, completely at sea.

Tony took a deep breath and calmed down, but his annoyance was still strong. "You got me all the way over here just to have a laugh at my expense. I can't believe you would think something like that was funny.''

Funny? Grant frowned and shook his head, feeling as though the ground was quaking out from under him. ''You met her?'' he asked, just to get something straight.

Tony almost growled. ''Yeah, I met her. And you know darn well she's not my type.''

''Not your type?'' Grant repeated, beginning to feel a bit annoyed himself. ''What was wrong with her?''

Tony gave a sigh of exasperation. ''Come on, Grant. We're wasting time. I've got things to do.''

Grant's expression was taking on a belligerent aspect. Jolene was just about perfect and he was beginning to resent Tony saying otherwise.

Michelle noted the look in his eyes and quickly intervened, pushing him gently back as she stepped to the forefront. ''Well, he had to try. Seriously, Tony, he thought you'd be smitten once you saw her. But who can predict the vagaries of human emotions?''

Tony caught himself up short and turned to smile at her. ''I guess Grant's changed more than one would think,'' he said to her. ''But you sure haven't.'' He shook his head, looking at her. ''You know, Michelle, we really ought to get together some time.''

She smiled up at him, her green eyes wary but softening. ''I'd like that.''

He nodded. ''I'd like Allison to get to know you,'' he said, looking distracted. ''I think you two would hit it off.''

Michelle's smile began to unravel along the edges. ''She's a lovely girl,'' she murmured.

''Yes.'' Tony nodded. ''She's so much like Mary was. But of course, she needs more older women in her life, women she can ask questions of, women who can guide her in ways I can't. So I try to call upon my friends to take a little time with her whenever possible."

"I'm awfully busy," Michelle said evenly, her face suddenly cool and distant again. "I have this job and I have—" her chin rose "—relationships."

Tony could tell he'd offended her in some way but he obviously wasn't sure how. "Oh, of course," he said quickly and he began to turn away. "I'm sure you do. Well, one of these days we'll have to..." A thought struck him and he turned back. "Say, what about Sunday?"

"Sunday?"

"Haven't you been invited to Mama's party? I hereby officially invite you."

Michelle looked from one brother to the other. "If it's just for your family..." she began.

"Hey, nobody's more family than you are," Tony told her. "Half the cousins are strangers compared to you." He grinned at her. "Come on over after church. Mama would love to see you."

Michelle dimpled. "I'll have to check my calendar," she mused, and they both grinned. The phrase harkened back to some obscure joke from their past, and it helped bond them again, a pale reminder of the unit they once were.

But that was all history, and Tony had to go pick Allison up. Turning, he clapped Grant on the shoulder with a large hand. "Make her come over," he ordered, seemingly over the experience of having taken a look at Jolene.

"I will," Grant promised gruffly, his eyes still stormy. He watched as Tony strode out of the restaurant the same way he'd come in.

"What do you think happened?" Grant asked out of the corner of his mouth as they watched him go.

"I don't know," she whispered back. "We'd better go in and find out."

The kitchen seemed normal enough. Picard was telling the Mexican busboys, who spoke very limited English, a long, complicated joke that they didn't get at all, and Jolene was using a pastry bag to pipe designs on the chocolate cake. She looked up as they came in, smiling as though she didn't have a care in the world.

Grant frowned and stopped before her, his hands shoved deep into the pockets of his slacks. "What did you do to my brother?" he asked bluntly.

Jolene looked up, startled, and inadvertently put a dab of butter-cream frosting on her nose. "What brother?" she asked.

"You know what brother," he said gruffly. "I only have one." But at the same time he reached out to rub the sugar concoction from her face. To do so, he had to step close, so close that he could feel her warmth, catch the light, sweet scent of her hair, and he felt a little light-headed. How could Tony have looked at this lovely woman and shoved her away? What kind of fool was he? Suddenly he realized he'd been standing too close for too long and he stepped back quickly, trying to keep the focus where it belonged. "I only have one brother," he said again. "Tony. What did you say to him?"

Jolene shook her head, bewildered. "I didn't say anything to him. I didn't even see him."

Grant stared at her. "That's crazy. He saw you. He said…"

Michelle quieted him with a hand on his arm. "I don't think so, darling," she told him softly. "Look over there."

He frowned and turned his head in the direction she was gesturing toward. There stood Fou Fou, happily shelling walnuts. Her bleach job looked worse than ever, the hair frizzy and the roots dark. She'd been working over hot water and her makeup had begun to run down her face. She looked like a clown who'd been left out in the rain. As he took all this in, Grant's eyes widened.

"Jolene," Michelle asked quietly. "Did you leave the room for any period of time in the last half hour?"

Jolene shook her head. "No, I don't think...oh, wait a minute. Yes, I did. Kevin was fussing and I went into the break room to play with him for a few minutes and to get him to lie down and take a nap."

Michelle smiled and turned to the older woman. "Fou Fou, did a tall, handsome man come in and talk to you a few minutes ago?"

Fou Fou looked up brightly. "Oh, yes."

Grant groaned softly. "And you told him you were the pastry chef, right?"

Fou Fou looked alarmed. "I told him a wrong thing?"

"You're the *assistant* pastry chef."

"Ah. Yes. Of course." Fou Fou was happy again and she waved a hand at them. "I will say that next time."

Grant's gaze met Michelle's and they both struggled to keep from letting laughter overwhelm them. Of course. That was it. He'd been so sure Tony would fall for Jolene, but if he thought Fou Fou was the woman Grant thought would be perfect for him, no wonder he'd been sure it was a joke. Fou Fou was a very nice person, but she was no beauty queen and definitely not Tony's type.

"What's going on?" Jolene asked, looking from one to the other.

"Nothing," Grant told her in a strangled voice. "Nothing at all."

But once outside the kitchen, he was sober and determined again. "That didn't work," he admitted. "But it wasn't really the fault of the plan. You can't guard against natural disasters."

"Ah, come on," Michelle teased. "Fou Fou may have her flaws, but she's no force of nature."

Grant slugged his fist into the palm of his other hand. "I can't believe Tony met the wrong woman," he grumbled. "We've got to think of something else." Suddenly an idea lit his face and he snapped his fingers, ending up pointing at Michelle. "The family party," he said.

She snapped her fingers pointing right back at him. "The family party," she echoed mockingly.

But he was too deeply involved to notice her mood. "Yeah, that'll get him. Once he sees Jolene in that setting, he'll know she's meant to be with us...I mean to be with him and Allison."

"Right," Michelle answered, but her voice was soft and rather sad and she watched as Grant walked off, his face full of concentration on his plans.

Six

"Big trouble," Jolene said mournfully as she and Mandy walked Kevin through the crisp fall air to the local park to play on the slide. "I think I might have to quit."

Mandy swung around and searched her face. "What happened?"

Jolene took a long, deep breath and looked around at the Christmas decorations being put up along the street. There was something so bittersweet about this time of year. Expectations got so high, and reality was often a letdown.

"I think," she confessed softly at last, "that I like him."

Mandy blinked and glanced toward where Jolene had been staring at the workmen putting up wreaths on the light poles. "Who?" she demanded.

Jolene sighed and turned her attention to her son, skipping on ahead of them, his little blue jacket with its cute little hood bouncing as he jumped over cracks in the sidewalk. "Grant Fargo," she admitted, wincing at the sound of his name as though it were a mortal sin.

Mandy made a face and looked perplexed. "So?"

Jolene gave her a sideways glance. "Don't you see how dangerous this could be?"

Mandy shook her head slowly. "No. I think it's nice you like your boss. I think that's the way it should be."

"Oh, Mandy, you know that's not what I mean."

Mandy stared at her for a moment, then rolled her eyes and laughed. "Honestly, Jolene, can't you like him without falling in love with him?"

Jolene shrugged tragically and looked away. "I don't know. I haven't had much practice at that sort of thing lately."

They turned into the park, right behind her son, and she looked back at her friend, her smile melancholy but mischievous.

"What if I can't?" Jolene said, only half teasing. "What if I start staring off into space at the sound of his name and imagining things? What if I start blushing when he comes into a room and shivering when he touches my arm?"

Mandy gave a mock laugh. "If that's the way you act when you're falling in love, I can see why you're worried. It sounds ghastly." She got stern. "Learn to control yourself. You're a creature of free will. You can do what you have to do."

Jolene nodded, dodging out of the way as two boys on skateboards came streaking past. "You're right," she said, squaring her shoulders and making herself strong. "I am woman. I am powerful. I can resist a man, no matter how handsome, how sexy, how nice and funny, how compassionate and caring..."

"Stop it," Mandy said, laughing. "I don't think this is going in the right direction. At this rate you're going to talk yourself into offering to work free, just to be near him.''

Jolene groaned, half laughing herself. ''You see what I mean? I'm in big trouble.''

Mandy swung around and took her by the shoulders, shaking her to get her attention. As she only came up to Jolene's chin level, it didn't make much of a dent in Jolene's composure, but she did stop and look down at her friend.

''What?'' she asked.

''Stop it,'' Mandy demanded. ''You said yourself this is the best job you've ever had. Don't mess this up. Think of Kevin.''

Jolene frowned. ''You're right.'' She bit her lip, then added, ''You know, I don't think he really likes Kevin very much.''

Mandy threw up her hands. ''There you go. How can you let yourself fall for a man who doesn't like your kid?''

Jolene nodded as Mandy turned to deal with helping Kevin onto the merry-go-round. ''That's exactly why I'm in big trouble,'' she muttered to herself. But as she watched her son, his little face shining with joy as he rode around and around with the big kids, she knew there was no contest here. Kevin came first. Always had, always would. And there was no way she was going to let anything as distracting as a man come between them.

''Men are scum and there's no getting around it,'' Mandy cried the next morning, waving a letter that had just come in the mail at Jolene as she munched on a breakfast muffin.

''Hey, watch that stuff,'' Jolene warned mildly. ''I'm raising a little man, you know.''

''Well, don't raise him to be a two-faced snake like

Stan," Mandy grumbled, sliding into a seat across from her. "In fact, I'd like to get a hold of the woman who raised this man and find out what she was thinking when she made him believe he was the center of the universe."

Jolene shook her head and swallowed her bite before responding. "No point to it," she advised casually. "All mothers raise their boys that way. Can't be helped. It's human nature."

Mandy tried to snarl but the effect was not particularly intimidating and Jolene ignored it. "So what has your man done that's got you all in a dither?" she asked.

Mandy's shoulders sagged. "He went ahead and left on that trip to Hawaii I told you about—the one I didn't want him to go on. And he left two days early without telling me to my face." She crumpled the paper in her hand. "He didn't have time to call, but he had time to write me a letter. How do you like that?"

Jolene waved a hand airily and made the appropriate sympathetic sounds. "Scum," she agreed. "You just can't trust them."

"Right you are," Mandy replied crossly. Then she looked anxiously at the clock. "He should have landed hours ago. Do you think he'll call?"

Jolene choked on her latest bite of muffin and turned, scarlet-faced, toward her friend, about to remind her of how angry she was supposed to be and how the sisterhood would handle such a situation with calm dignity, yet unassailable strength of will, but the doorbell rang before she could get a word out.

They looked at each other. "Who could that be?" Jolene asked as she rose to answer the door.

Mandy shrugged. "It's a little early for the UPS delivery man," she mused.

"It's Saturday, anyway." Jolene turned back at the last

minute. "Do you think it might be flowers from Stan to apologize?" she suggested.

Mandy shook her head. "No chance. He's probably waiting in his hotel room for an apology from me for making him feel guilty about leaving the way he did."

Jolene grinned. "You're right. Now aren't you ashamed of yourself?"

The doorbell sounded again and she grimaced. "I guess I'd better open it up and see who it is," she said, though she didn't sound eager. Reaching out, she turned the knob, and there on her doorstep stood Grant Fargo.

"Oh," she said as she stared at him.

"Hi," he said, smiling at her with cheerful charm. "I was out running at the track and I thought I'd stop by. Since I was in the neighborhood."

"In the neighborhood," she echoed blankly. "Oh, I see."

She'd never seen him this way before, so casually attired in a tracksuit and running shoes, his hair slightly disheveled by the wind. He looked younger, more devil-may-care, as though he couldn't possibly be the owner of a major restaurant, or even working in one. Suddenly she found herself smiling back at him.

"Come in," she said quickly. "Please..." She stood back and glanced at the living-room area to see if it was tidy or if she would have to distract him in some way and scurry around to clean the place up. For once, it looked relatively neat. She sighed with relief and smiled at him again, closing the door and gesturing toward the kitchen table.

"Meet Mandy. I know you've talked to her before but I don't think you've been formally introduced. She's my roommate."

He turned toward Mandy and held out his hand.

"She's also in mourning," Jolene went on. "Her boy-friend just left for Hawaii." She knew she was babbling but she couldn't seem to stop at the moment. First she was tongue-tied, now this. "His name's Stan. He's a fashion photographer and he took along a boatload of super models." He was looking at her strangely and she had to go on. He seemed to expect it. "She thinks he'll return a changed man. She begged him not to go."

Mandy nodded sadly, though her eyes were twinkling at the sight of her friend so nervous. "I did try to get him not to go. But he said I'd have to get used to this if there was to be a future for our relationship."

Grant gave her a crooked grin as he sat down on the chair she'd kicked out for him. "Is there going to be one?"

Mandy looked surprised. "One what?"

"A future?"

"Oh, for our relationship?" She laughed. "Doubtful. I'm not getting used to it. And deep down, I don't really want to."

Grant nodded sympathetically. "I can't even imagine getting used to it."

"Then you're on my side?" Mandy asked pertly.

He put out his hand again, and she took it. "I'm with you all the way."

Mandy laughed as they shook on it, and when she turned to Jolene, who'd sat down to join them after getting a fresh coffee mug and a carafe of coffee for Grant, she announced, "Hey, Jolene, I like this guy. And you told me he was so cold and ruthless."

"Mandy! I did nothing of the—"

"You told her what?"

They both voiced outrage and Mandy laughed. "Come on you guys," she protested. "You can't take me literally today. I'm dealing with a broken heart and serious withdrawal pangs. I'm just a little giddy.''

"Don't worry," Grant told her soothingly as he wrapped his hands around his coffee mug. "I'll find you someone new. A better guy. One who gets airsick and won't travel."

"You?" she asked wonderingly, knowing he was mostly joking, but not sure if there wasn't a grain of truth to his words. "Why would you do that?"

He shrugged. "I'm getting into this matchmaking stuff. If all goes well with my current project, I'll see what I can do for you."

Mandy stared at him, bemused and Jolene shook her head. She had no idea what was going on or how they got on this subject. She was still nervous. It had been a long time since a man had come to call, and it had been even longer since one as attractive and appealing as this one had shown any interest at all. She had to admit, she liked it. But she knew she wasn't supposed to.

"Where's the kid?" he asked, turning to her.

"His name is Kevin," she said, correcting him automatically. She'd done it so often by now, it was practically a running joke between them. "He's asleep." She nodded toward the bedroom just off the living room, which she shared with her child. "He was up late last night playing peekaboo with Auntie Mandy."

"Oh, sure," Mandy said, trying to look pathetic. "Blame it all on me."

"It's all her fault," Jolene told Grant obligingly. "It always is."

They all laughed, though Mandy did drop her head to the table and bang the flat of her hand on the surface, pretending complete dejection. But she was laughing too hard to pull it off and when Grant suggested getting a cup of water to throw on her to stop the hysteria, she gave it up quickly enough.

"What I actually came for," Grant said when they'd all calmed down and refilled coffee mugs all around, "was to invite you to my mother's house tomorrow afternoon. She's having a big family party. I'd very much like you to come."

He looked directly into her eyes and for a moment, she was lost there. His gaze was so dark, so clouded with mystery, she wanted to reach out and touch him to make sure he was real. She restrained herself, but her heart was beating faster, pounding in her chest as though something was going to happen and she had to be ready. *Defense,* she told herself silently. *Don't let emotion take over.* Carefully, deliberately, she pulled back and gave herself a mental shake.

"Oh," she said again. It seemed to be her favorite word today. "Uh, well, I don't know how I can. I have so much to do...." Her voice trailed off as she tried to think of a good excuse to skip it.

"Maybe if Mandy comes, too?" he suggested, looking questioningly at her friend.

But Mandy shook her head. "I've been hired to run my pretzel machine at the Santa Claus parade in Montrose tomorrow afternoon," she said. "But thank you for asking."

Grant turned back to Jolene. "Michelle will be there," he told her. "And my brother, Tony."

His brother, Tony. Warning bells were beginning to go off in her head whenever he mentioned Tony. There always seemed to be such significance in the way he said the man's name, and yet she didn't have a clue why that might be. Before she could respond to what he'd said, Mandy's jaw dropped and she turned to look at Grant.

"No way. You're not Tony Fargo's brother." She reacted to his nod. "Why didn't I connect the names before?"

"You know my brother?" Grant asked as though he were delighted.

"No." She shook her head solemnly, then, realizing how airheaded she sounded, she added quickly, "I mean, not now. But years ago, when I was just a kid, he was one of my brother's best friends."

Grant frowned, studying her face. "Who was your brother?"

"Hank Lawton."

His frown cleared. "Oh, yeah, I remember him. Good tennis player."

Mandy nodded, pleased. "Real good. He's even ranked nationally."

"No kidding?"

They chatted about old times for a few minutes, then Grant turned to Jolene again. "The party starts about three and goes forever. You can come anytime. Or if you'd like me to pick you up..."

By now she was shaking her head, her heart in her throat. "No, I'm sorry Grant, but I don't think I can make it. I've got a million things to do and..."

His huge dark eyes took on a doleful look. "My mother will be hurt," he told her, somehow making it seem a very important point.

"Oh." She hesitated.

"My mother's Italian and when she throws a party, she cooks for days ahead of time. She's been cooking special things for you. You can't disappoint her."

Jolene looked to Mandy for support. "But..."

"Besides, Kevin would love it. My father bought Mama one of those old-fashioned mansions down on Orange Grove when his restaurant took off." He handed her a card with the address. "There's a whole playland in the back-yard, filled with swings and a train he can ride and me-chanical birds hanging from trees making a racket. He'll have a ball."

Jolene hesitated. For the first time, she was tempted, even though she knew how risky it was going to be to do this. "Well…"

He rose to go. "We'll expect you some time after three, okay?"

"Well…"

"Great. See you then." And he was gone before she'd really decided. She stood staring at the door he'd just closed, wondering what she should do. It might be fun. On the other hand, she didn't want to get any closer to Grant. It was too dangerous. She turned to get Mandy's advice, but her friend was staring into space and shaking her head.

"I remember Tony, all right," she was murmuring. "He was gorgeous and really, really nice."

Jolene groaned and dropped back into her chair. "So I've heard. Athletic, too. And brainy as all get-out." She threw up her hands. "In fact, I haven't heard one discouraging word about the man. Isn't there anything bad you can tell me?"

Mandy tried hard, her brow furled, but she couldn't come up with anything. "It's been a long time," she said defen-sively. "Surely he's done something unsavory or illegal by now. It's just that I don't know about it."

Jolene grimaced and looked away. "You're no help. The man is too good to be true. I hope I never meet him."

Mandy's eyes sharpened as she gazed at her friend. "Meeting Tony Fargo is the least of your worries," she noted wisely.

Jolene's head whipped back so that she could see Mandy's face. "What do you mean by that?"

Mandy leaned forward on her elbows, her chin in her hands. "Working with Grant Fargo is your problem," she said, nodding. Her eyes narrowed as she mulled that over. "And I'm beginning to see why it scares you so."

Jolene opened her mouth to respond, then closed it again. What was there to say? She was right.

"Now he's planning to introduce you to the members of his family." Mandy made her eyes widen in mock horror. "Look out."

Jolene made a face at her friend but didn't protest. She wasn't sure how much of this was just the typical Mandy dramatics and how much was for real. "What does that mean?" she asked.

Mandy spread her hands out on the table and looked long and meaningfully into Jolene's eyes. "It means he *really* likes you," she said, enunciating slowly as though to make it perfectly clear.

"Well, sure but…" It began to dawn on her what Mandy meant. "Oh my God."

Mandy held up a hand. "Hold on, don't get crazy. Really liking is nice. It isn't really threatening."

Jolene wasn't mollified. "What if I start *really* liking him back?"

Mandy thought for a moment, then offered, "You don't have to."

Jolene's shrug was eloquent. "But I've already got tendencies in that direction," she explained.

Mandy put her chin back in her hands. "Hmm," she said. "You win. You're in big trouble."

Seven

Grant entered his mother's kitchen and immediately felt completely at home. Various aunts and cousins sat around the long central table, some folding napkins, one shelling peas, another rolling cannelloni, every one of them talking. Two uncles stood in the doorway arguing politics, their voices getting louder and louder to be heard above the fray. Most turned as Grant entered and called out a greeting, and one young, dark-haired cousin jumped up and kissed him on the cheek. His short, plump mother was busy cooking lasagna noodles, her pretty face tense with concentration as she tested for doneness. Her big old silver Persian cat looked up from his perch on the stool at the end of the kitchen and blinked his green eyes at Grant, meowing silently. A teakettle screamed as steam shot out through the spout. A buzzer went off in the oven. Someone began to sing a raucous popular song. In other words, the place was embroiled in chaos.

Grant grinned. "Ah, home sweet home," he muttered looking around at the familiar faces with pleasure. He would no more allow his kitchen at the restaurant to go nuts like this than he would allow rats in the storeroom. But at his mother's house, it felt right and natural.

He greeted relatives and friends with a joke here, a congratulations there. He stopped to pet Mr. Slippers, the Persian cat, and got bit on the thumb for his efforts, making him yell, which scared the cat, who flew away like an enraged ball of silver fur, and brought all the younger females into the room hurrying to his side to exclaim over the little spot of blood and to bind his wounds. Finally he worked his way back to his mother. She'd dumped out the lasagna noodles by now and was trying to pry them apart. He grabbed her around the waist and kissed her, making her giggle.

"Mama, guess what," he whispered into her ear. "I found a girl for Tony."

His mother lifted her flour-dusted face to give him a look of horror and shook her head severely. "No, you don't, Grant. You cannot give your brother one of your old girlfriends. That would be...that would be..." She couldn't think of a word vile enough to express her outrage.

Grant laughed and hugged her. "No, Mama. She's not one of my girlfriends. She's not like that. She's a very nice girl."

His mother sniffed at him suspiciously. "Well I'm glad you still know the difference," she muttered as she went back to pulling the sticky fat noodles apart.

Grant ignored her words. It was an old argument and he knew he'd never win it, not with his mother. "Did you make a nice panettone like I asked you to?" he said instead. "I told her you were making something special for her visit and I don't want to be a liar."

She turned and looked into his face, and stared hard as though she were looking for the sweet boy she'd raised.

"You can't manipulate people like chessmen," she told him bluntly. "You start making up things and tricking those you love and you'll come to no good end." She shook her forefinger in his face. "You be good, Grant. And work on your own self. It's no use you trying to find someone for Tony. He'll never get over Mary."

"Mama, Mary was great." Grant reached past her and grabbed two black olives, which he popped into his mouth as she tried to shoo him away. "She was beautiful and about the nicest person who ever walked the earth." He frowned at her earnestly. "But Mary isn't here anymore. And he needs someone."

His mother paused, staring into memories of the past and let what Grant was saying sink in. "I know," she said sadly at last. "And Allison needs a mother." Reaching up, she patted her younger son lovingly on the cheek. "But, Grant, honey, Tony has to find his own way. You can't do it for him."

Grant's rebellious look had been minted in this very kitchen about thirty years before and time hadn't dimmed it. "If we leave it to him," he protested, "he'll end up married to his television set. We can't let that happen. He's got too much to live for."

His mother cocked her head to the side, looking him over. "And you, my darling. When are you going to start living a real life?"

Grant's grin was back. "Hey, give me a break," he complained. "I'm living as fast as I can."

She nodded, giving him a significant look. "Too fast. That's the trouble. You need a wife and you need to start a family."

A shadow darkened his eyes. "Mama, I tried. Remember Stephanie?"

She snorted derisively. "Marrying Stephanie wasn't trying," she said shrewdly. "Marrying Stephanie was giving up."

Grant turned away. He didn't want to talk about Stephanie, especially not with his mother. Stephanie was a closed chapter in an old book, but talking about her opened things up again and all that came from it was pain.

Luckily there was a diversion that got him off the hook. Someone was coming up the walk. The arrival was announced by a flock of children dashing in through the kitchen door and screeching, "Aunt Rosa, come quick. Somebody's here."

Now, the house and yard were filled with people, so this was hardly unusual. The fact that the children found it so meant the newcomer was a stranger, at least to them. They jumped up and down and demanded her attention to the matter.

Grant's mother shooed them out of the kitchen, but in the meantime, Grant took a look out the window, turning back with a grin. "Here she comes, Mama. The girl I told you about. Look at her. What do you think?"

His mother came next to him and stared out the window. Jolene was dressed in blue slacks and a white sweater, looking rather nautical, and her silver blond hair was flowing free around her shoulders, giving her an ethereal aspect. It was a nice combination, he thought. Whatever—she just looked darn good to him.

She had Kevin by the hand and was making slow progress toward the front door. Kevin was stopping to smell the flowers and then to point at a bug. Grant couldn't hold back a chuckle. At this rate, dinner might be over before they actually arrived.

But Rosa frowned as she studied the two of them from inside the window. "She's got a little boy with her."

"Yeah, Kevin. He's her son."

His mother gave him a sharp look. "She was married?" she asked. "She's divorced?"

He hesitated. That was something he didn't really know for sure. He knew what she'd told him, but it had been sketchy at best. It hadn't occurred to him that his mother wouldn't approve just because of something like that. "Divorced," he said shortly. Wasn't that what she'd said?

Rosa rolled her eyes. "You want this woman to marry your brother and you don't know anything about her," she cried. "You'd better do some research, my darling one. You're being much too cavalier with your brother's happiness."

She was right and he knew it, but then, she didn't know Jolene the way he did. Jolene was a straight arrow, true blue, one of a kind. Integrity radiated from every pore. She was just about perfect. Or else she was a damn good actress.

There was no time to puzzle out the truth, for suddenly she was in the room and smiling at everyone. People cooed over Kevin, who basked in the glow, his little round face alight with unselfconscious joy, and Jolene handed a wrapped box to Grant's mother.

"A cheesecake," she told her. "I thought maybe you could use one with all these people."

Rosa looked at her suspiciously before accepting the box and thanking her coolly, while Grant frowned, thinking his mother could be a bit more gracious with her gratitude and regretting he'd told her about his plans.

"Jolene is a pastry chef, Mama," he said quickly, hoping to swing the appraisal in her favor. "Her cheesecake will melt in your mouth."

"That's nice." Rosa put it to the back of the counter as though it were something she meant to pack away with the heirlooms. "We'll see if we need it."

When pigs fly, Grant thought, recognizing the stubborn light in his mother's eyes. But before he could protest, there was a cry from across the room, and when they turned, black smoke could be seen billowing out of the oven and those at the table were leaping to their feet.

"Oh, no. The chicken's burning! Look out!"

Jolene's instinct was to run to the rescue, but Grant pulled her, along with Kevin, from the kitchen and into the living room. When she looked up, she found him laughing.

"The chicken," she protested, pointing back toward where the commotion was coming from and shaking her head at his attitude. "The fire."

"It happens every time," he told her with a grin. "Believe me, there are enough people in that kitchen to take care of it." He began to guide them toward the French doors that would lead them outside. "That's one reason so many of them are hanging around in there. My mother has a well-deserved reputation for burning dinner."

"Oh, come on," Jolene said, giving him a quizzical look. "There was good food all over that kitchen—beautiful pans of lasagna, sausages and peppers grilled to perfection, cannelloni, pizzas…"

"All brought by cousins and aunts and friends," he told her as they stepped out onto the brick patio. The sweet, pungent scent of flowers hit him like a steady breeze and he frowned, looking around the yard. It wasn't spring. What could be blooming? Then Jolene turned and her hair brushed his shoulder and he knew. That lovely scent wasn't flowers. It was Jolene.

He had to make a determined effort to step away from her and lose the sensual wave that was trying to wash over him. With effort, he remembered what he'd been talking about. "Uh, Mama's never been much of a cook. It was my dad who did all the cooking when I was growing up."

Jolene nodded, oblivious to his reaction. Turning slowly, she took a moment to survey the scene. The lawn seemed to go on forever, bordered by oaks and redwoods that gave it a woodland meadow aspect. Girls in bright dresses were playing near the trees. A group of men were tossing horseshoes. A young couple was strolling, hand in hand, around the edges of the lot.

"Your father had the restaurant before you, didn't he?" she murmured, her mind more on the scene spread out before her than on his words.

He nodded, and despite everything, he couldn't help but notice the way her silvery hair settled on her shoulders, then tumbled down her back as if it were a wild stream flowing down a canyon. The navy blue slacks looked crisp and efficient and the lacy white top looked soft and alluring and all in all she looked delicious.

But he wasn't supposed to be thinking things like that. "He ran the restaurant from before I was born," he said, trying to get back to reality. "I took it over when he died."

She took a few steps toward the grass and looked around in wonder. "So this is the atmosphere you grew up in?" she asked, comparing it silently to her own less sumptuous beginnings. She flashed him a teasing smile. "No wonder you're spoiled rotten."

He slapped his hand over his heart. "Guilty as charged. I had a great childhood. If I went into therapy I'd have a hard time finding anything to tell the shrink. Any mistakes I've made can be laid squarely to my own front door."

She turned and looked up at him and he looked down at her and something in their gazes locked for just a moment. Jolene's heart began to pound, but Grant was pulling away,

frowning. He glanced down and caught Kevin looking up
at him out of the corner of his eye.

"Hey," he said, grateful for a diversion. "Look at your
son. He's plotting something against me."

"What?" Jolene laughed as she reached out and put a
hand on top of Kevin's blond head. "You're getting para-
noid. He's just a baby."

"Yeah? I've heard that one before. 'He's just a baby.'"
His eyes narrowed as he stared down at him. "And yet I
have a feeling he's really a forty-year-old man in a baby's
body."

Kevin gave him a grin he could have sworn was mock-
ing. The boy's sharp little baby teeth seemed to glisten
wickedly at him. Grant frowned uneasily.

"And besides, like they say, just because you're para-
noid doesn't mean someone isn't chasing you," he reminded Jolene.

She reacted with more laughter. The things Grant said
often struck her as funny. "What?" she demanded.

He gave her a sassy, superior look and raised an eyebrow. "Never mind."

She turned away because she wanted to reach for him,
give him a hug. That impulse wasn't all that new, either.
Day after day she worked with the man, and day after day,
she liked him more and more. There was something so
appealing about him. He seemed very lovable. Not that she
was going to let herself actually *fall* in love. But a hug or
two wouldn't hurt, would it?

But she managed to hold back the urge and turned away
instead and when she did she saw the family pet lying on
a flat rock a few yards away. "Oh, look, Kevin," she said,
pointing it out to her son. "Look at that beautiful cat."

Kevin's eyes widened. "Kitty!" And he was off, his
little legs moving like chubby pistons as he dashed across

the grass toward where Mr. Slippers was stretched out in the sun. "Kitty, kitty, kitty!"

Jolene had only just barely opened her mouth to call out a warning to Kevin when Grant took off, running up behind the boy and grabbing him around the waist like a rag doll just before he reached the cat.

"Not so fast, young man," Grant told him, swinging him up into his arms. "The kitty doesn't like kids a whole lot."

Kevin reacted with shock, then outrage, kicking his feet and squirming with all his might, trying to get away. "Kitty!" he called out, reaching toward where the cat was staring at him with malevolent green eyes and lashing her silver tail.

"No kitty," Grant insisted, holding him firmly but gently. "Stop it, Kevin."

There was something in the deep male voice that seemed to send a warning through the child's frame. He quieted, looking up into Grant's face warily.

"Look at this," Grant told him, showing him his own thumb. "See where the kitty bit me? I don't want him to bite you like that."

Kevin stared, fascinated, at the small tooth marks on Grant's thumb. "Kitty," he murmured very softly.

Jolene caught up with them and put out her arms. Grant dropped her child into them. But the moment Kevin realized he was no longer under Grant's supervision, he began to kick and fuss again, his hard little shoes making painful jabs against her legs and Jolene had a hard time holding him. Turning back, Grant took the child from her again.

"Oh, no, Grant," she said, alarmed. She knew Grant wasn't overly fond of children—or at least not this one, and she wasn't sure what he was about to do. "I can handle him. Really..."

But Grant merely dropped into a chair and held Kevin

until he calmed down, then set him up where he could look down into his angry red face.

"That's unacceptable, Kevin," he said firmly. "You are not allowed to treat your mother like that. Do you understand?"

Kevin stared up at him, his blue eyes filled with rebellion, his mouth in an exaggerated pout. Suddenly the chin was thrust out and the mouth opened and a long strand of meaningless jabber issued forth, obviously meant to be a direct response proclaiming how little he cared about Grant's opinion.

Jolene stepped forward, ready to snatch her baby away from Grant before he did what came naturally after a challenge like that, but Grant warned her back with a quick shake of his head and he went on speaking to the boy in a cool, firm voice and holding him with a steady gaze.

"I want you to promise me, Kevin. You will never kick your mother again. Okay?"

Kevin's bravado seemed to evaporate. He looked at his mother, then back to Grant.

"Tell me you will never kick your mother again. Say 'okay.'"

Kevin swallowed hard and nodded. "'Kay," he muttered in his gruff little man voice.

"Good boy," Grant said, and pulled him close for a quick hug. "Now go run and play."

He set him down and without hesitation Kevin's little legs started taking him in the direction of Mr. Slippers. But the cat, older and wiser than most, had been watching the entire proceedings and seemed to know what he was in for if he stuck around. The moment he saw Kevin coming, his ears flattened against his head and he took off like a silver shot, disappearing into the woods.

Luckily there was a big red ball on the ground right

behind where the cat had been and Kevin was immediately distracted. A group of teenage girls came streaming out of the house at the same time, and in a moment, they'd surrounded him, and he was in center-of-attention heaven.

Grant and Jolene chatted while they watched him charm the girls, but Jolene's mind was on what had just happened. There were times when she felt a lot of remorse over the lack of a father in Kevin's life, and the way Grant had just handled the situation with the tantrum Kevin had been working up to proved the point. Here was a man who knew next to nothing about children, but he had the instincts of a father. He'd done it just right. If only...

But she shook that thought away. Her situation wasn't ideal, but it was what she was stuck with and she would make the best of it. Still, there was no doubt about it, a child was meant to have both sexes in his life. It was just like her grandmother used to say. *You need a mom for tea and sympathy and a dad for power and perimeters.* Not that the two couldn't blur and blend. But the roles came down pretty well defined, and that's what kids needed. They had to have something to rely on, people they could count on come rain or shine.

Kevin would always be able to count on her. She'd made that pledge to him the day in the hospital when she first held his little red, scrawny body in her arms and cried tears of joy that landed on his wispy hair. The next sixteen years or so were dedicated to him, and she was not going to forget it, no matter how tempting other things got.

Another flock of young people came bursting out of the house and spread across the grass. She looked up and marveled. "This party is getting bigger all the time," she murmured, mostly to herself.

Grant looked around quickly, hoping Tony had arrived, but not finding him among the crowd. A couple of men waved to him and some girls smiled, but Tony's face was not among them. Three young women detached themselves and came over.

"Hi, Grant," said a redhead, grinning and cracking gum while she swung a racket from one hand to another. "We need a fourth for badminton. You want to give it a try?"

"Badminton." Jolene laughed softly. "I was league champion in badminton my senior year in high school."

"No kidding?" the girl said, delighted. "Then why don't you come play?"

Jolene turned back toward Grant, the look in her eyes hopeful but undecided. "Oh, I can't. That was years ago. I..."

"Sure you can," Grant told her, smiling at her reluctance. "You're here to have fun. Go on. I'll take care of Kevin."

"Really?" She was tempted, no doubt about it. It had been a long time since she'd swung a racket at a bird.

"Great," the redhead chirped. "Just come on over to the badminton court when you're ready." And she started off with the other two.

Jolene looked after them, chewing her lip. What the heck. Why not? She turned back to Grant with a shrug. "Who are all these people?" she asked, gesturing toward the young women she was about to play with.

"Cousins," he told her blithely. "Italian cousins. What can I say? Don't bother to try to learn names. I never have. Go and have some fun."

"Kevin..." She swung around to look at him but Grant waved her off.

"I'll handle him."

She took a deep breath and felt a sudden rush of freedom, even if for only moments. "Okay," she said, her eyes brightening. "Let me go show these women what competition is all about."

She gave him a cocky wink and he laughed as she strode off toward the court. Turning, he found that Kevin had left the group of kids he'd been letting admire him and was heading purposefully across the grass. Turning further, he spotted the objective. Mr. Slippers had come back out from the trees and was diligently washing himself, sitting on a stepping stone.

"Oh, no, you don't," he cried, heading Kevin off at the pass once again. This time the child laughed as he swung him around. "Scat!" he called to Mr. Slippers, and the cat disappeared into the bushes. He set Kevin down and grinned at him. Kevin looked back. He wasn't grinning himself. He looked on edge and a little wary, as though he was ready to jump and run if Grant made any sudden moves.

Grant had to laugh. He hadn't realized a little boy could be so very...well, so very male. There was a certain bond between them, no matter what.

"Okay, Kevin," he said to him. "It's you and me. What do you want to do?"

A gleam appeared in the boy's crystal silver-blue eyes. "Cookie," he said firmly.

Grant hesitated, but then nodded. "Okay. I wanted to go to the kitchen anyway. Let's see if we can find you a cookie."

He took Kevin's hand and found it sweeter to hold than he'd supposed. In fact, he felt downright warmhearted taking the little guy for a walk this way. It put him in such a good mood, he was almost sanguine enough to deal with his mother once they found her.

And that wasn't easy. For once, she wasn't standing at the sink, doing something with food. He glanced around

NO RISK, NO OBLIGATION TO BUY...NOW OR EVER!

GUARANTEED

PLAY "ROLL A DOUBLE" AND YOU GET FREE GIFTS! HERE'S HOW TO PLAY:

1. Peel off label from front cover. Place it in space provided at right. With a coin, carefully scratch off the silver dice. Then check the claim chart to see what we have for you – FOUR FREE BOOKS and a mystery gift – ALL YOURS! ALL FREE!

2. Send back this card and you'll receive brand-new Silhouette Desire® novels. These books have a cover price of $3.50 each, but they are yours to keep absolutely free.

3. There's no catch. You're under no obligation to buy anything. We charge nothing – ZERO – for your first shipment. And you don't have to make any minimum number of purchases – not even one!

4. The fact is thousands of readers enjoy receiving books by mail from the Silhouette Reader Service™. They like the convenience of home delivery...they like getting the best new novels BEFORE they're available in stores...and they love our discount prices!

5. We hope that after receiving your free books you'll want to remain a subscriber. But the choice is yours – to continue or cancel, any time at all! So why not take us up on our invitation, with no risk of any kind. You'll be glad you did!

THIS SURPRISE MYSTERY GIFT COULD BE YOURS <u>FREE</u> WHEN YOU PLAY "ROLL A DOUBLE"

"ROLL A DOUBLE!"

place label here

SCRATCH HERE

SEE CLAIM CHART BELOW

225 CIS CDWH
(U-SIL-D-01/98)

YES! I have placed my label from the front cover into the space provided above and scratched off the silver dice. Please send me all the gifts for which I qualify. I understand that I am under no obligation to purchase any books, as explained on the back and on the opposite page.

NAME _____

ADDRESS _____ APT. _____

CITY _____ STATE _____ ZIP _____

CLAIM CHART

 4 FREE BOOKS PLUS MYSTERY BONUS GIFT

3 FREE BOOKS PLUS BONUS GIFT

2 FREE BOOKS

CLAIM NO.37-829

The Silhouette Reader Service™ — Here's how it works:

Accepting free books places you under no obligation to buy anything. You may keep the books and gift and return the shipping statement marked "cancel." If you do not cancel, about a month later we'll send you 6 additional novels and bill you just $2.90 each plus 25¢ delivery per book and applicable sales tax, if any.* That's the complete price — and compared to cover prices of $3.50 each — quite a bargain! You may cancel at any time, but if you choose to continue, every month we'll send you 6 more books, which you may either purchase at the discount price...or return to us and cancel your subscription.
*Terms and prices subject to change without notice. Sales tax applicable in N.Y.

If offer card is missing write to: Silhouette Reader Service, 3010 Walden Ave., P.O. Box 1867, Buffalo, NY 14240-1867

BUSINESS REPLY MAIL
FIRST-CLASS MAIL   PERMIT NO. 717   BUFFALO, NY

POSTAGE WILL BE PAID BY ADDRESSEE

SILHOUETTE READER SERVICE
3010 WALDEN AVE
PO BOX 1867
BUFFALO NY 14240-9952

NO POSTAGE
NECESSARY
IF MAILED
IN THE
UNITED STATES

quickly through the relatives assembled at the table, looking for Tony, but saw no sign of him. There was, however, a whole plate of cookies for Kevin. He installed him next to an aunt, then followed the sounds of cans falling as they led him into the pantry where Rosa was trying to find more ingredients for more most likely inedible dishes she was planning to cook.

She didn't hear him come in and as he gazed at her, he decided it was no use to try to get a conversation going. She had a look on her face that he recognized from too many past experiences. She was upset, and he was afraid he might have some idea of why.

He'd wanted to ask her what she thought of Jolene, but he could see it would be a very bad time. When she had a bee in her bonnet, it was usually best just to let it buzz. He turned, hoping to leave as silently as he'd come, but she turned at the same time and saw him.

"Grant, carry these cans for me," she asked, gesturing with an armful of stewed tomatoes and tomato paste. "I'm dropping them everywhere."

He took them from her, but when he glanced at her face, he could see a lecture coming on. Groaning, he stopped and leaned against the doorway. "Okay, Mama," he said, a martyr going to his doom. "What is it?"

"She has very weird eyes," his mother said without preamble.

He turned his head and looked her in the face, controlling himself. "They're beautiful," he replied, holding back his outrage at her judgment.

She shook her head. "No. They are very strange. They make her look strange." She shrugged. "Like some kind of wild animal. Tony does not like strange girls. I think you should give that up right away."

Anger was surging through him and he knew better than

to respond to what she'd said. Better to keep his mouth shut. If he let her know how he felt, she would banish him from the house.

"The little boy has those strange eyes, too. I think you should stay away from them both."

That was just too much to bear. "What do you think, that she's a witch?" he demanded. "That she's some kind of vampire or werewolf or something, just because of her eyes?"

His mother sniffed. "Of course not. I don't believe in such things."

"Then what? You think she's some kind of 'bad girl' because she has silver eyes?"

"I'm not saying what I think." She began to push her way past him. "I'm just saying that you should keep her away from Tony." She stopped as she came next to him. "She's no Mary," she said bluntly.

He winced. "Mama, there is no Mary. She's gone. No one can replace her."

She looked up at him and snorted. "Especially not this one." And then she was gone.

Grant stayed for a moment longer, working on reining in his temper. The injustice of his mother's opinion ate away at him. She didn't even know Jolene, didn't know how sweet she could be, how funny. She would be perfect for Tony. Why couldn't anyone else see that?

When he finally made his way back into the kitchen, he found Kevin at the counter trying to weasel another cookie out of his mother, who was resisting. His first reaction was to defend the boy, to make sure his mother wasn't being mean to him. But what was he thinking? His mother had never been mean to a child before. Why would she start now?

"You see?" he said to her from one corner of his mouth. "He's darn cute, isn't he?"

She looked at him and relented a little. "Yes, he's definitely adorable," she admitted reluctantly. "But he's got to go," she added quickly. "He can't be in the kitchen. It's too dangerous here. He could get burned."

A crack about her cooking reputation was on the tip of his tongue, but luckily, he swallowed it. "Okay," he said, looking down at the towheaded child. But before he could corral him, a group of prepubescent girls descended like a swarm of locusts.

"Oh, isn't he cute!" they shrieked, dancing around him. "Oh, I love his hair. I love his eyes. Look at his cute little arms."

"Uncle Grant," one cried. "Can we play with him?"

Grant paused and gave that a little thought. "You want him?" he asked at last.

The girls' mouths dropped open and their eyes popped. "Are you giving him away?" one of them breathed.

Grant nodded stoutly. "To the highest bidder."

The girls giggled, realizing it was a joke, and Rosa scolded Grant.

"Gina and Amanda, take Kevin over to the play yard and give him a ride on the train. Keep him out of my Iceland poppies, but let him play just about anyplace else." She gave her son a look of exasperation. "Grant can't seem to understand what little boys want." She rolled her eyes at him. "You'd think you'd been born fully grown and ready to drive a car, for heaven's sake. Don't you remember childhood at all?"

The girls went off, Kevin gurgling happily between them, walking on chubby little legs, and Grant, relieved to be rid of the responsibility for the moment, looked out at the street. "Where's Tony, anyway?" he asked. "When did he say he would get here?"

"He said he'd be a little late," Rosa responded, scrubbing a pan out with steel wool. "Allison has a soccer game."

He twitched impatiently. "And when do we eat?"

"Half an hour," she said firmly.

That meant about an hour and a half, he thought to himself, but that hardly mattered. All he was here for was to put Jolene and Tony together and see how they got along. He was getting itchy to get it over with. Somehow he wasn't looking forward to it the way he had in the days leading up to this party.

Eight

Grabbing a carrot from the bin, Grant wandered out onto the grass, looking toward the badminton court where Jolene seemed to be returning everything that came her way with a vengeance.

He paused nearby but not near enough to be noticed, watching her. She had the grace of a cat, the athleticism of a natural athlete and a competitive spirit that came as something of a surprise to him. He moved closer, enchanted by the way she played.

She was leaping into the air, going for a high shot, and suddenly, as though he'd planned it, he found himself reaching out to catch her, like plucking a bird in flight out of the sky. She landed hard against him and they both fell, slipping backward, his arms around her, her hair whipping across his face. She cried out and he laughed, holding her longer than necessary, holding her close and feeling her warmth, her strong, slim body.

They both struggled to their feet, helping each other, both laughing now. The girls came over and called out encouragement, then coaxed Jolene back into the game to finish up her point. But he didn't pay any attention to what was being said. He could still feel her against him, still smell her scent and taste her hair. She was growing on him and it was Tony who was supposed to be feeling this way.

"Tony," he muttered to himself. "I've got to get her to connect with Tony in some way."

"Where's Kevin?" she asked when she'd finished and was joining him to stroll across the grass.

"Some of my younger cousins have him," he told her, pointing out where Kevin could be seen through a break in the trees, bounding from one piece of play equipment to another with a bevy of girls in tow.

Jolene smiled to see him so happy. She looked up at Grant and somehow he was included in her warm glow. She had the urge to take his hand in hers, but before she could follow it, he gestured toward the house. "Kevin will be okay for a few more minutes," he said, looking down at her with veiled eyes. "Come with me. I want to show you something."

She followed him into the house and up a long, winding staircase. He led her down a dark, carpeted hall to a doorway, where he turned and said, "Tony's room," as though that was supposed to mean something to her.

"Oh?" she said politely, wondering why she should care.

"Let's go in," he said, pushing the door open and stepping slowly into the room.

"Why?" she asked, lingering stubbornly in the hallway. This obsession Grant seemed to have with his brother was beginning to bother her.

He looked back in surprise. "Because I want to show

you something," he said, switching on the light. "All Tony's trophies and awards are in here. Come on in and take a look."

She lingered for another moment, feeling contrary, but he was already surveying the room with satisfaction and she didn't want to ruin his fun. She sauntered in slowly just as he turned and looked at the other side of the room.

"Hey," he said, startled by what he saw. "That's my old bed. And my dresser. My mother must have moved all my stuff in here with Tony's."

She had to laugh at the outrage in his face. "Neither one of you use this room anymore, do you?" she asked.

"No," he admitted, scowling. "But that's not the point."

"Oh, for heaven's sake. You *are* a spoiled brat." She dropped onto his bed and drew her legs up, watching him with the interest of a student of human nature. "My old room has probably been bulldozed down by urban renewal projects, but you don't see me shedding tears."

He looked down at her smile, saw the dare in it and thought she was the cutest thing he'd ever seen. "I'm not shedding tears," he protested gruffly.

"Oh, no," she teased, laughing up at him. "Just whining a little, are you?"

He took a step toward her, wanting to accept her challenge and take her in his arms, but then he realized where he was and why and he stopped himself abruptly, spinning on his heel and going back toward Tony's side of the room.

"I just wanted to show you some of Tony's things," he told her, forcing a cheerful tone. "Look here. This is Tony's football trophy. He was all-league that year."

Tony's football trophy didn't interest her in the least. She looked around at the shelf behind the bed where she was sitting and pulled down a trophy with a swimmer poised at the top. "What's this?" she asked him.

"What?" He turned back with a frown.

"This trophy here?" She waved it at him. "It seems to have your name on it."

"Oh. That was for swim." He dismissed it with the wave of his hand. "But Tony's was for football. He was a defensive end but—"

"I like yours," she said, looking it over. "I like swimmers better than football players any day."

He looked nonplussed for a moment, as though she'd gone off the track and he wasn't sure how to get her righted again. He turned back to Tony's things for support.

"Oh, hey, I'd forgotten all about this one. Look." He brought an old photograph over for her to examine. "Tony's old Corvette. It was completely thrashed when he bought it and he fixed it up himself. It won Best of Show out at Ontario Speedway."

"Really." She glanced at it only long enough so that she wasn't being rude, then looked behind him at a picture that stood in a golden frame on the desk. "Who is that?" she asked.

He turned to see what she was looking at and time seemed to stop for a moment. Stephanie stared back at him, looking just as lovely as ever and his heart gave a thump before he steadied himself. "That...that's Stephanie," he told her. "I was married to her once."

Jolene noticed the catch in his voice and she nodded. "Oh, she's so pretty," she noted softly.

And she was. She looked like an angel, her hair settling around her like a mantle, her eyes dreamy, her lips slightly parted. She had a face that would be easy to love and hard to forget. Jolene glanced at Grant and wondered. He was still standing there, staring at the picture.

"How long were you married?" she asked him, her heart sinking a little. It was obvious the woman still had an emotional hold on him.

He turned and looked at her as though he'd forgotten she was there. "Six months," he said shortly, putting Tony's picture of his Corvette away.

Her eyes widened. "Whoops," she said.

Suddenly he grinned. "Yes, it was a whoops."

She smiled back at him, glad he'd lost that haunted look he'd worn for a moment. She would have liked to have gone on to something else and never spoken this woman's name again, but she knew that wouldn't make her disappear from his mind—and maybe his heart. Better to get things out in the open.

"What happened?" she asked softly.

He tried to smile in a carefree way but he couldn't quite pull it off. "Oh, the usual," he began, but then a strange thing seemed to twist inside him and he found himself doing something he'd never done before—he began to tell the truth about Stephanie and why she'd left him. No one else knew. He wasn't sure if that was because it hurt too much at the time to tell anyone, or because he was ashamed. But he hadn't been able to tell anyone, not even his mother. And now he was telling a woman who was almost a complete stranger, and feeling compelled to spill it all out.

Somehow he ended up sitting beside her on the bed. Their shoulders were touching and he was telling her about how Stephanie had expected married life to be one long party and how disappointed she'd been when she'd realized more would be required of her than to spend his money as fast as she could. She'd opted out quickly enough. Some of her friends were leaving on a cruise of the Caribbean and she wanted to go.

"It sounds as though she was just too young," Jolene murmured sympathetically.

"It was more than that," he told her. "It was just as much my fault. I found out I wasn't suited for marriage."

"Then," she added.

"Anytime," he responded, surprised at how good it felt to unburden his soul to her this way. "Some people are just meant to be alone and I'm one of them."

She didn't believe that and certainly didn't like it, but she didn't tell him so. Not yet.

"So tell me," Grant said, changing the subject at last as he leaned back against the wall and looked at her. "What happened to Kevin's father?"

"Well, I will tell you," she said. She'd known her turn would be coming and she was prepared. "Kevin's father heard the age-old call of the wild, and he had to answer. He was seduced by those northern lights, the mystery, the danger. He longed to return to the days when men were men and roughing it meant living at one with nature at her cruelest." She paused and let a smile tease him. "He's an actor. He's doing little theater in Anchorage, Alaska," she said at last, making him laugh, which was exactly what she'd wanted to do.

"You're not married to him?" he asked, just to make sure.

"Not anymore."

She turned to look into his face and as she did, her hair brushed his cheek and suddenly there was a strange buzzing in his ears. His gaze met hers and locked, lost in the silver mist of her beautiful eyes, and he had to ball his hands into fists to keep from touching her.

She sensed his reluctance and didn't know why he felt it. They were so close, sitting on the bed. She could have melted against him if he'd let her. She wanted to. But something in his face told her it wouldn't work and she bit her lip and looked around for something to distract them, pulling a book down off the shelf.

"And what's this?" she asked.

He blinked like a man waking from a dream and frowned at it. "Nothing. Just an old yearbook."

"Really?" This might just be a find. "Your high school yearbook?"

"Leave it. It's boring." He tried to regain the enthusiasm to bring her closer to his brother. "Come look at Tony's."

"No, thank you," she said wisely, leaning back against the pillow and beginning to flip through the yearbook. "I want to look at this. Mind if I read the letters?"

His frown was deeper. "Yes, I do."

"Aw, come on," she coaxed, looking up at him with a teasing smile. "Old yearbooks are fun."

"Old yearbooks are embarrassing."

She laughed softly. That was exactly why she liked them. "So many years ago," she murmured as she turned pages. "It must all seem like a dream to you now."

"More like a nightmare," he growled, but he stayed beside her and looked over her shoulder.

She found a picture of him with long hair and another in his swimsuit, making her laugh and him squirm. Finally she began to read some of the letters.

"'Stay as cute as you are.' Wow, that's inventive." She stole a glance at him. "But she was right. You were awfully cute."

His eyes smiled at her. "I'll bet you were cuter."

She threw back her head and laughed out loud. "You'd lose that bet. I was scrawny and awkward and I was always dropping my books, especially in front of boys I had a crush on."

He grinned. "I know the feeling. My voice always cracked just when I was trying to be cool and debonair."

"Oh, here we go," she said, pouncing on a letter written in purple ink. "This one's got a little more pizzaz. 'My darling, hunky Grant, remember all those hot nights behind the stadium and the time you pulled off my...'"

"Hey!" He made a grab for the book. "No way! Who was that?"

She held the book to her, laughing and not letting him see, trying to hold him off with a straight arm. "No, wait. You have to hear the whole letter first."

He wasn't sure whether to laugh or be outraged. "You're making it up."

"Am not."

"Are, too."

"Let me read the rest."

"No!"

He grabbed for the book again and she turned away, dropping back against the pillow. He came after her, wrestling for the book, which she wasn't giving up. Clinging to it and laughing, she twisted to get away, but he had her pinned with his long body, and before she knew it, his face was so close to hers, she could feel his warm breath on her mouth and the book slipped away without her even noticing.

He didn't notice, either. She felt so soft and firm and round and hard and sweet and challenging—he knew he was going to kiss her. It was only a matter of time, and when his mouth came down on hers and felt it open and melt beneath his touch, his heart seemed to turn in his chest and he lost the sense of his surroundings, lost all sense of time, all logic, all judgment. He only wanted her, all of her, in his arms, in his bed...

She tasted like roses smelled, all deep and dusky and as

rich as thick honey and he wanted to drown in her. His
hands tightened on her and his tongue drove more deeply
into her mouth. He didn't know if he was searching for her
soul or establishing mastery. It was all part of an age-old
urge between man and woman and his body was a part of
it now.

She was spinning out of control and she knew it, but she
was too elated to make it stop. She'd wanted this for so
long. A man's arms, a man's touch, a man's mouth on hers,
she needed it like the way a child needed praise. It would
feed her, sustain her, make her whole again. At least for
the moment.

But more than that, she wanted Grant. He had her lost
in confusion the way he seemed interested, then pulled
away, awakening senses in her she'd thought she'd pushed
down and smothered, only to find them springing to the
surface when his gaze met hers, or his hand brushed her
shoulder. She came alive when she was near him. She
didn't know what it all meant, but she knew she liked it.

His kiss was wild and hot and made her breath stop in
her chest. Somewhere in the distance, she heard someone
calling that dinner was on the table, but her mind wasn't
processing words at the moment. She was completely immersed in feelings, and when he finally pulled away, she
heard a whimper of protest and realized it was coming from
her own throat.

"How did I end up with you in my arms?" he asked her
wonderingly, leaning on one elbow above her, his free hand
trailing a path between her breasts and coming to rest over
her stomach, where his fingers spread and he held her as
though she was worth protecting. "I was just going for the
yearbook, wasn't I?" He seemed truly bewildered.

She stretched luxuriously, loving the feel of his hand,

and smiled up at him. "I don't know," she said softly. "Maybe it was just meant to be."

He stared down at her, shaking his head, his eyes so deep she couldn't tell if he were smiling or angry. Carefully, as if he didn't want to cause attention to be paid, he withdrew his hand from her belly.

"What is going on?" he murmured, still perplexed and moving impatiently. "Are we having a lunar eclipse or something?"

She touched his cheek with her hand. "It's the gravitational pull of the Earth."

He took her hand in his and brought it to his lips, kissing her palm so softly, it was like a breeze. "That's tides," he told her huskily.

She sighed happily. "Maybe we're like tides. We're just being pulled together."

He stared down at her for a long moment, then grimaced as he realized what it was he was doing here. "No." He pulled away, looking pained. "This isn't right."

She propped herself up with her elbows and looked at him as he rose from the bed and backed away. Here it was again, the rejection that came whenever she seemed to get too close. She didn't understand it, and it was beginning to make her angry.

"I'm sorry," she said stiffly. "I didn't mean to intrude upon your space."

He turned back, shaking his head, his face a mask of conflict. "No, it's not that, it's just that..." He started to reach for her again, drawn inexorably and relentlessly toward her by something he couldn't explain—and couldn't let happen.

"Oh God," he muttered, pulling himself back with all his strength. Turning, he took a deep breath and steadied himself.

"Say," he began, his voice impossibly hearty. "Did you know Tony was a presidential scholar?"

She threw the pillow at him, threw it hard enough to knock him off balance, bounded off the bed and headed for the door.

"Wait a minute," he said as he grabbed her arm and stopped her. He was half laughing, half woeful, and as she looked up into his face, so was she, though she managed a look full of reproach at the same time.

"Okay, that was clumsy," he admitted. "I take it back."

"And you'll never show me any of Tony's trophies again?" she demanded, only partly joking.

He glanced back at Tony's things on the shelf with regret in his eyes. "But…"

She narrowed her eyes warningly. "Promise?"

He scowled. "Oh, all right."

She brightened. "Okay, I forgive you."

She was laughing up at him, her eyes glowing, her lips so soft, and he couldn't resist. *Just one quick kiss to seal the bargain,* he thought irrationally. *Just one.*

His lips touched hers and something seemed to flow between them, something with the kick of a shot of whiskey and the heat of a sunbeam. He wanted more and he began to pull her close, but the door to the room swung open and his mother's voice ripped into his heavenly dream and tore it to pieces.

"The food is getting cold," she said calmly, but when his head shot up and swung around and he met her gaze, he saw the condemnation in her eyes. "Better come on down and get some."

They both stood frozen where they were as she turned and set off down the hallway. Jolene looked up at Grant and found him swearing harshly under his breath. Once again, she didn't get it. He was a grown man in his thirties.

What did he care if his mother found him kissing a woman? It didn't make any sense.

He took her hand and led her downstairs. They didn't say much to each other. *As though we were kids found making out in a parked car,* she thought to herself, puzzled. But they loaded their plates high with food and went outside to watch Kevin play while they ate. After a few bites Grant excused himself and went inside to talk to his mother, and Jolene couldn't help but wonder. What was he saying to her? And why?

"Mama, listen..." was all he could get out at first.

His mother's outrage knew no bounds. "You *are* trying to palm off one of your girlfriends on Tony. I knew it! This takes the cake, Grant. Of all the low, sneaky, under-handed..."

"Mama, will you just listen?" Grant rubbed his temple. He definitely felt a headache coming on. "It's not like that. It's...it's too hard to explain right now, but it's not like that."

She lifted her nose in the air and harrumphed.

Groaning, he shook his head. "Mama, just tell me this. When is Tony going to get here?"

A light of triumph lit her dark eyes. "He already came," she told him calmly.

He glanced around the kitchen. "Where is he?"

"Gone again."

"What?"

She nodded. "He came with Allison and they ate while you were...upstairs. Then they left again, with Michelle."

He blinked. "Michelle was here?"

"Yes. But Allison had a report on ghosts due at school in the morning and Michelle knew someone with a haunted house, so they went out there and—"

"Damn!"

"Grant, no swearing in this house. You know that."

He nodded, his expression pained. "I know that, Mama. And I'm sorry." He started to back out of the room, still talking. "And I'm sorry about kissing girls in your house, too." He saluted her as he hit the doorway. "And about everything I've ever done. Forgive me, Mama," he called back as he let the door swing shut behind him.

She looked after him, frowning. Maybe she shouldn't have been so hard on him. He was the one she worried about. Her youngest. Her baby. If anyone should find a nice girl, it should be him.

And of course, he had found a nice girl, but he'd found her for his brother. Unfortunately, that whole concept was pretty hard to explain, even to his mother.

He rejoined Jolene and finished his meal, but he seemed distracted, and finally she couldn't stand it any longer. She was pretty sure she knew what was bothering him, the only thing she didn't know was, why?

"Grant," she said at last as they were strolling around the yard to look at the Iceland poppies bobbing their colorful heads in a corner flower bed. "Why was that so wrong?"

He didn't need an explanation. He knew exactly what she was talking about. Now he just needed an excuse, and grasping at straws, he found one.

"Uh, I'm your boss. I, uh, it's not right to try to have a relationship when we have to see each other every day at work." He looked into her infinite eyes and had to look away. Surely she could see he was full of baloney. "I mean, what if it didn't work out?" he added rather lamely.

"Are you serious? Is that really all it is?"

He steeled himself to meet her gaze. "I'm quite serious. I'm really a believer in not mixing business and pleasure."

She searched his eyes, then asked softly, "And was it a pleasure?"

He grimaced. He couldn't lie to her. "You know it was," he said, his voice low and gruff.

She nodded, satisfied, and turned to continue their walk.

When it was time to go, she thanked Rosa and got only a perfunctory smile. Then Grant helped her load her sleeping baby into the car seat and stood beside her car in the gathering darkness to say good-night.

"We had a wonderful time," she told him. "I'm glad you invited us."

"I'm glad you came," he said gruffly, his hands shoved deeply into his pockets as though to make sure he didn't touch her.

She looked at him and shook her head. "I guess I can't expect to get a kiss good-night," she teased him. "You'll be afraid I'll ask for a raise in the morning."

He couldn't help but smile back at her. "I guess I could risk it," he told her reluctantly. "I've always been one to live on the edge."

She reached up and they touched lips, just for a moment. The kiss was so soft, it might almost have been in their imagination.

"Good night," she whispered, drawing away and turning to get into her car.

He didn't say anything, but he stood and watched as she drove off. And he was still standing there, with his hands still in his pockets, long after her taillights had disappeared from sight.

Nine

Mandy came in to wake Jolene early the next morning. She knocked softly, opened the door a crack, then came bounding in and jumped up on the bed like a friendly puppy.

"Wake up, Jolene," she insisted in a loud whisper. "I've got the greatest idea. I've been up since three thinking about it and I can't wait any longer to tell you."

Jolene opened one eye and peered at her sleepily. "What time is it?" she muttered blearily.

"Uh, half past six. It's early, I know, but my idea…"

Jolene blinked at her, her face scrunched in wake-up agony. "Is Kevin awake yet?"

Mandy had the grace to look contrite. "Uh, no."

Jolene's hands shot up and grabbed Mandy's shirt by the lapels. "You woke me up and Kevin's not even awake? Do you realize what you've done?"

Mandy swallowed hard and tried to smile. "A wise man once said, early to bed and…"

"Benjamin Franklin was never a mother," Jolene wailed, letting go of Mandy's shirt and thrusting her head under the pillow to drown out Mandy's voice. "Sleep, precious sleep," she murmured into the covers.

Mandy hesitated only a moment, then pulled the pillow away. "When you hear my idea, you'll forget all about sleep," she insisted.

"That already happened the day I had Kevin," Jolene moaned, rolling from side to side with her hands over her ears. "When you have a toddler you have to grab every minute of downtime you can."

"I'm serious, Jolene. Listen to me. Listen."

Jolene stopped rolling but her eyes were shooting daggers as she stared up at her friend.

Mandy went into her sales pitch with enthusiasm. "Are we not good-looking women, on the whole?" she asked perkily.

Jolene frowned at her. "We're passable, I guess," she began, but then she turned her head and caught sight of her tousled reflection in her dresser mirror and she groaned. "At least I thought I was before I went to bed. Something must have happened in the night."

Mandy managed to bounce while still sitting down. "Come on, we're both great looking and you know it, you with your silver eyes and me with my long legs."

"Long legs? You're five foot two!"

"Well, cute legs. I've been told I have cute legs. Often."

Jolene grimaced. "So we're knockouts. What is your suggestion, that we become ladies of the evening or go looking for foreign princes to marry?"

"No, my dear. This is perfectly legit and moral. We'll become—" she paused for dramatic effect "—models."

Jolene frowned, not sure she'd heard correctly. "Models? What are you talking about?"

"We'll work as models. We'll apply together and we'll be a pair. We'll make scads of money and at the same time, I'll be able to go on assignments with Stan."

Jolene stared at her, appalled. "You woke me up for this?"

Mandy looked hurt. "Don't you think it's a good idea?"

Jolene stared harder. "In a word, no."

"Jolene, it's fabulous. We're not young girls. I just read an article that says the modeling market is crying for women like us. We'll be the hit of..."

Jolene closed her eyes and groaned aloud. "Mandy, you're too short to be a model."

Mandy hesitated, her lower lip trembling just a bit. "I could do petites."

Jolene sighed, reaching out to take her hand and going to a more sympathetic tone. "Even petites are taller than you, at least they look it." She shook her head. "Mandy, things always look very weird in the middle of the night. I think this idea is one of those things. Have a cup of coffee and think it over in the light of day."

Mandy's face took on a stubborn look. "You think this is just a jump out into the blue, but I know the modeling business. I worked with models when I was in the garment district. I know what I'm talking about. You've got to have an angle to set yourself apart from the thundering herd. We could be a mismatched pair."

Jolene closed her eyes and grimaced. "Don't be ridiculous. I'm not modeling."

"Oh, come on, Jolene." She gave her friend a coaxing smile. "It would be more fun if we did it together."

Jolene was finally coming fully awake and as she did, she was more perplexed than ever that her roomie would even bring up such an outlandish idea. "Mandy, I'm a pastry chef and I've got a wonderful job."

Mandy's face drooped and her eyes, only moments before full of eagerness, dulled. "I know. I just feel so..." She shook her head and let it drop. "I don't know what I was thinking. Modeling just seemed a perfect way out. I've done some myself in the past, you know."

Jolene was surprised to hear it. "You have?"

"Sure. I've done hand modeling." She put up her pretty, slender hands to show Jolene. "See?"

Jolene frowned as she studied her friend. Slowly it dawned on her what this was all about. "Oh, Mandy. You can't get over him, can you?"

Mandy's face quivered. "No. I can't seem to." She sighed, all the air going out of her dreams. "I could begin to sing, like one of those girl groups from the sixties, about chains of fools and all that. But the truth is, I just can't stop thinking about him."

Jolene smiled sympathetically. "To the point where you would even give up pretzels?"

Despite everything, Mandy laughed. "Yeah, I think so. I just can't get rid of the guy."

Jolene took her hand and held it tightly. "I know. In fact, I know exactly how you feel."

Mandy hesitated. "You mean...?"

She nodded ruefully. There was no point trying to run from the truth any longer. The afternoon with Grant, despite all the strange things he did, had sealed her fate. She could no longer just wonder what it would be like to be in his arms. Now she knew.

Her grandmother used to say, "Don't fall in love, darling. It only complicates things." And, as usual, her grandmother had been right. But it was too late to listen to wise advice.

"I'm a goner," she said softly.

Mandy's eyes widened. "You're in love with Grant?"

Jolene looked pained. "Well, if it's not love, it's a darn good imitation of it."

"Go slowly, Jolene." Mandy's face was troubled. "You've got more than just yourself to think of."

"Don't I know it?" Jolene shook her head, and at the same time, sounds coming from the other side of the apartment announced that her son was ready to greet the day. "And that's why I might have to give him up."

Mandy took her hand again. "What are you going to do?"

Jolene shot her a quick, brave smile, gave her a hug and rolled out of bed, heading for Kevin's room. "Not become a model, that's for sure."

"Hello, traitor."

Michelle looked up from the books as Grant entered the restaurant office and for just a moment there was a guilty light in her eyes. "Hi," she said faintly.

He leaned against the desk with his arms folded, looking down at her coolly. "Haunted houses, Michelle?" For a moment, his eyes burned. "You came in and grabbed my brother and his daughter and took them to a haunted house?"

Michelle tried gamely to smile. "But I do know someone who has ghosts. Irv Bickel. You remember him, don't you? All sorts of things go on in his place. Doors slam and things slide across the counter and there's moaning. There's a whole history to it. You see, in 1892..."

"I don't want to hear about it."

Michelle cringed just a bit. "I'm sorry if I ruined your plans," she told him softly.

He shook his head, his gaze troubled. "I thought they were *our* plans. I thought you cared about Tony."

Her face cleared. "I do. I care a lot about Tony."

Grant frowned, looking puzzled. "Then don't you want him to be happy?"

Michelle turned her gaze away and swallowed hard before answering. "With all my heart," she said softly, her voice muffled.

Grant shrugged, his anger beginning to fade. "Well, maybe we can salvage something out of this. Did you tell him about Jolene? Did you tell him how wonderful she is?"

Michelle looked at him and stifled a smile. "No, Grant, I did not tell him that."

He frowned again, thinking strategy. "When are you going to be seeing him again?"

She shuffled papers on the desk to keep from looking into his eyes. "As a matter of fact, I'm going to dinner with him and Allison Thursday night."

"Ah, one of those throw-a-mature-woman-at-the-kid things, huh? You can tell him all about her then."

Michelle looked up for a moment, and if Grant had been paying attention, he might have noticed that her eyes flashed at his words. But she kept her voice even as she answered him. "Actually we did talk about her a little, in a roundabout way."

"Really? In what roundabout way?"

She rose and went to the file with a stack of papers. "Tony has a friend who's getting married Saturday," she told him as she worked. "The bakery where he ordered the wedding cake just burned down, so I suggested..."

"You told him Jolene would do it," he guessed quickly, springing away from the desk, already excited. "Michelle, that's great."

She looked at him and smiled. She'd known him all her

life and he seemed almost like a younger brother to her. No matter how much he annoyed her, she couldn't really be angry with him—especially when he gave her a bear hug and practically danced her around the room.

"I told him I'd talk to you about it," she stated, pushing his exuberant affection away.

"Okay," he called back over his shoulder as he left the office. "You've talked to me. Now let me talk to her."

Jolene wasn't in yet and he paced the restaurant, and then the kitchen, waiting for her, his mind full of plans. Then she walked through the door and his plans grew muddled, because she wasn't the woman he was busy preparing for his brother; she was the woman he'd kissed the day before, and that made all the difference.

"Hi," she said, walking right up to him with a teasing look in her eyes. "Don't worry. I won't mention yesterday."

"Yesterday?" He tried to smile.

She bit back her grin. "That's it," she said in a loud whisper. "You just stick to that story. 'Yesterday? Never heard of it.' That ought to do it." She waved a finger at him. "No one will ever know."

If he wasn't careful, she was going to make him laugh. He turned, watching her put away her things in the cabinet. "Jolene, I remember yesterday very well," he said softly, knowing he was treading on dangerous ground.

"Oh, yeah?" She looked into his eyes for a moment but she didn't see what she'd hoped for and she turned away again. "Then why don't you hum a few bars?" she cracked, turning to set up Kevin's playpen.

He was afraid he knew what she'd been looking for. He'd made a big mistake the day before and now he was going to have to work his way back out of it—if he could.

Reaching down to help her with the playpen, he tried to think of a way to mend things.

"Jolene, we need to talk," he began, but Picard came in carrying Kevin and Fou Fou cried out a greeting and the place seemed to come to life. Grant lapsed into a watchful silence, waiting for things to calm down again.

It took a while. Everyone seemed to have something to say to Jolene. As he watched, one employee after another came to her, patted Kevin's head, exchanged friendly words with Jolene and moved on. In a few short weeks, she'd made herself indispensable there. Her smile lit up the place. And more than that, it lit a flame in him.

That wasn't supposed to happen and he was going to make sure it didn't show. No one would ever know. Least of all Jolene.

"Okay," she said at last when things had settled down. "What was it you wanted to talk about?"

He took a deep breath and prepared to launch into his topic, but unfortunately, at that very moment, Kevin spied him. "Cookie!" he called, banging his little fist on the top of the bar to his playpen. "Cookie!"

Grant stopped, looking pained. He turned to Jolene with a questioning look. "Does he have to call me Cookie all the time?" he complained.

"That's how he first knew you," she explained with a twinkle in her eyes. "He just naturally attaches the name to you."

He saw the twinkle and let his shoulders relax. That was the way he should take it, as she did. There was a way to find humor in everything, he supposed. Even this. He turned and looked at the boy. "But we've been through so much more together since then," he said lightly. "Maybe he could call me something new."

"You should be pleased. After all, he likes cookies."

She laughed softly. "Just be glad he's not calling you Green Jell-O. That's another favorite of his."

Grant grinned. He couldn't resist it. Her amusement was contagious sometimes. "There's a distinction you know," he told her sagely. "Green Jell-O is the king of the Jell-Oes."

She looked at him and laughed, suddenly able to imagine him at about seven, eyes wide as he contemplated a huge bowl of the jiggly stuff. "I'm sure it is," she agreed.

He moved closer, enjoying her laughter. This was better. Keep things light. He didn't really have to discuss any of this with her. It would come naturally if he just relaxed and let it happen.

"Okay, here's the deal," he told her. "How would you like to bake a wedding cake? I know someone who needs one."

"A wedding cake?" Her eyes widened and her hand went to her mouth. Her surprise was complete and it made him smile to see it. "Oh! I've always wanted to do a wedding cake. When do they need it by?"

"Saturday," he told her. This was fun. He wished he knew more ways to make her this happy.

"Saturday? Ohmigod. I'd better start planning right away." Excitement lit her face. "How big is it supposed to be? How many servings? Do they want a tiered cake or not? What colors? What filling? Do they want a groom's cake, too? There are so many things to plan!"

She turned, focused, but slowly a frown began to grow between her eyes and she turned back, looking suspicious. "Wait a minute. Who is it for?"

Grant smiled guilelessly. He'd hoped to avoid this question until a little later in the process. "A friend."

Her suspicions grew. She took a step back toward him. "What friend?"

Grant shrugged and tried to look innocent. "You've never met him."

Her eyes narrowed as she studied him. She was getting to know him well enough to have an instinct for when he was trying to avoid telling her something he knew she didn't want to hear. "Grant, I want to know. Who is this wedding cake for?"

Michelle walked in as she was asking the question. "Didn't Grant tell you?" She smiled at Jolene thinking she would be pleased with her answer. "It's a friend of Tony's who's getting married. Tony will be handling all the details."

"Tony?" Jolene turned and pinned Grant to the wall with her glare. "Tony?" She took a deep breath, shaking her head. "Oh, that's just great. I thought we had a deal." Her eyes flashed. "Why don't you bake it yourself?" Turning on her heel, she took off toward the kitchen.

Michelle was aghast, turning to Grant with questioning eyes. "What did I say?"

Grant groaned, shook his head gloomily and sank into a chair. "It's my fault. I've turned her against Tony."

Michelle's eyebrows rose in surprise. "How did you manage to do that?"

"Never mind. It's a long story." He waved a hand in her direction. "There's only one way to fix things. I'll make sure Tony picks up the wedding cake on Saturday. And I'll make sure Jolene is here when he does."

Michelle pursed her lips, looking in the direction Jolene had disappeared in her huff. "That is, if you can convince her to make it."

"I'll convince her," he promised dolefully. "It won't be easy, but I'll convince her."

Michelle decided not to leave things to chance. Later that evening, she snagged Jolene and led her into the office, sat her down across the desk and let her know what she wanted to get across right away.

"Jolene, I want to explain to you about Tony."

"Grant's brother?" Jolene just barely caught herself before she rolled her eyes. "What's to explain? He's the most wonderful guy in the world. I've heard all about it."

Michelle gave her a perfunctory smile. "No, you haven't heard all about it. There are reasons that Grant acts the way he does about Tony. Old reasons. Things that go way back to when they were growing up."

Jolene stared at her for a moment, then relaxed against the back of the chair. "Tell me more," she said quietly.

"Tony was the older brother, always getting good grades and doing what was expected of him. Grant was the baby of the family..."

"Always messing up and getting in trouble," Jolene finished for her, a smile in her voice. She'd sensed that in him from the beginning. "That's pretty typical."

"Maybe," Michelle countered. "But in their family, it sometimes seemed to go a little too far. And the thing was, though their mother managed to love them both equally, their father...well, he showed a marked partiality to Grant."

Jolene frowned, horrified. "Oh, no. Why would a father do such a thing?"

Michelle shrugged. "Joe was pretty much of the old school. He didn't have a lot of tact. He made it pretty clear he thought Tony was a stick in the mud, and that he thought Grant was just like he had been when he was young. Kind of wild, very adventurous, sort of devil-may-care."

Jolene thought about that for a moment. She liked imagining Grant as a youngster. "He's not really like that now," she noted.

Michelle nodded. "Everyone's got to grow up some-time," she said.

Jolene smiled. "But you can see traces of his old ways in him from time to time. I have to admit, I find it rather attractive myself."

"Do you?" Michelle didn't smile. Instead she studied Jolene's face as though she thought she might find some-thing out—something she needed to know. "Well, when you meet Tony, just remember that Grant has a real need to make it up to him."

She frowned, still not altogether clear on this. "You mean, make up for the fact that their father favored Grant?"

Michelle nodded again. "That, and other things. Grant adores Tony. Always has."

Jolene laughed. "Now that is pretty obvious," she ad-mitted.

"So when he asks you to bake this wedding cake..."

Jolene's head came up and her gaze cooled. "Oh, so that's what this is all about," she said. "Did he send you to butter me up?"

Michelle's wide mouth gave a small twist of annoyance, but Jolene didn't notice.

"You can tell him I'll think about it," she said. "I'll think long and hard. But I'm not promising anything."

"Thanks for hearing me out," Michelle said a bit wea-rily, rising from behind the desk. "I've got to get back to work."

"Me, too," Jolene responded, but with a frown. She knew something was bothering Michelle but she didn't know what. Surely it couldn't be this thing about Tony and Grant. Could it? But if not that, what? She wished, belat-edly, that she'd kept her mouth shut and just listened to what Michelle had to say.

As she followed the woman back into the kitchen, she

realized she had a decision to make. Would she bake the wedding cake, or wouldn't she?

In the long run, she couldn't resist. She'd taken a class in wedding cakes in culinary school, but the cake they'd built had been by committee. This time she was going to be in charge and doing most of the work herself. It was exciting, challenging, and she hardly cared who the cake was for after all.

"Five tiers and a pedestal," she was heard to murmur as she leafed feverishly through her reference books, constantly consulting the list of the bride's instructions Grant had carefully left lying in plain view. "Let's see, the foundation layer will be constructed of four ten-inch rounds. The next layer will be fifteen inches, then thirteen, then ten, then the pedestal, then a seven-inch. The whole thing will be...my God, over twenty inches wide and thirty inches tall!"

"Can you do it, Miss?" Fou Fou asked her anxiously as she hung behind her, twisting her apron in her hands.

Jolene threw her a wild-eyed look. "I have to do it, Fou Fou." She stood up and faced the entire crew, her hands balled into determined fists. "I have to, and I will."

The kitchen staff cheered, Picard waving his butcher knife in the air, and she marched into the office with head held high to find graph paper and plot out the decorations. Grant watched, amused, as she lost herself in designs and drawings, only coming out of her trance when Kevin called her.

Everyone stood ready to help her and she commanded them like a general going to war. She had Fou Fou mixing bowl after bowl of cake batter and had Picard testing the oven temperature at intervals and the busboys cutting out cardboard rounds for support. She baked two versions of each layer, picking the most perfectly formed, coating each with apricot glaze, encasing them in plastic wrap and freezing them in the big wall freezer.

"Not only to keep them fresh," she explained to Grant when he questioned her about the need for freezing. "It's also so that when they cut the cake, it won't crumble."

On Friday things reached fever pitch. Jolene didn't seem to hear much that was said to her. Her mind was completely on the task at hand. By late evening, she was finalizing plans for the decorating and had Fou Fou as busy as a bee, mixing one enormous batch of cake frosting and five other batches of decorator frosting, each batch in a different color.

"What's the difference between the frostings?" Michelle wanted to know, sneaking a taste when Jolene was looking in the other direction.

"The cake frosting is smoother for easy application," she responded mechanically. "The decorator is thicker and creamier in order to hold its shape as I force it through the pastry bag."

"I'm impressed," Michelle remarked to Grant, because Jolene wasn't really paying attention any longer. She was holding a bowl of pale violet decorator frosting up to the light, trying to decide if it was quite the right shade.

"You and me both," Grant told her softly. But he lingered, watching how immersed she was and feeling a little neglected. It had been days since they'd shared a joke or a comment. He hadn't realized how much he'd come to depend on her to fill up his days with laughter. Reluctantly he left to make his rounds of the tables and check on how the evening meal was going.

Jolene didn't even notice. She was practicing forming the roses by the hour, staying much later than she'd ever stayed before. "I want to get them just right," she told anyone who asked. The final versions were made on wax paper affixed to the top of a small jar. She turned the jar slowly with one hand while squeezing pale pink frosting out of the pastry bag with the other, forming wafer-thin petals, one upon another, until a perfect rose was created.

"Aah," breathed Fou Fou when she saw the results. Thirty-five pale pink and violet roses sat ready to go on the cake. "As lovely as the real thing, no?"

Jolene smiled. There was nothing like the feeling of having made something with your own hands and having it turn out to be wonderful. The only thing better was...

She turned quickly, realizing she had forgotten all about Kevin for ages now. The playpen was empty. Her heart jumped in her throat and she sprang up, panic sizzling through her like a lightning bolt. But the sounds of childish laughter stopped her in her tracks. Relief flooded her and she walked softly up to Grant's office and peeked in.

There were the two of them, Grant and Kevin, sitting on the floor, rolling a ball back and forth across the carpet. She watched for a moment before they noticed her. Kevin was laughing his little boy laugh that seemed to gurgle out of his throat like a spring and Grant was grinning at him, his eyes soft and kind and happy. Warmth filled her and so did something very dangerous, something much too close to hope.

"Hey," Grant said at last, catching her eye and smiling. "Look, Kevin. Here's your mom."

Kevin barely noticed. He rolled the ball and squealed with delight.

"Thanks," she said to Grant. "I was so busy, I..." She shook her head, letting it go, her shoulders sagging. "Anyway, I've got to take Kevin home and give him some dinner."

"He's already eaten," Grant said, nodding toward a plate on the desk. She could see the remnants of meat and mashed potatoes. ''I tried to tell you I was feeding him but you were too involved to hear me.''

Guilt swept over her. Not only was she ignoring her son, but she was ignoring her boss as well. Not wise. But more than that, not kind, and she wanted to show Grant only kindness. The longer she knew him the more she thought he deserved it.

''Grant, I'm so sorry,'' she began, but he waved her apologies away.

''We had fun,'' he said, rising to his feet and smiling down at her. She did look tired. He glanced at the clock, knowing this was much later than she usually stayed. ''But you'd better take him home and get some sleep. Tomorrow is the big day.''

She nodded. The deadline was at hand and the cake was going to be assembled and frosted the next day. ''I'll be in at six in the morning,'' she told him. ''I want to leave myself plenty of leeway in case anything goes wrong.''

''Nothing will go wrong,'' he told her confidently. ''You've been magnificent. You've done this very carefully and I know it will all come together and be the most beautiful wedding cake there ever was.''

She laughed, pushing her hair back behind her ear. He seemed to be saying all this so earnestly and it was so exaggerated. ''Can I get that in writing?'' she asked lightly, though her eyes looked a bit cloudy. ''That way I could take it out and read it on bad days, just to get my spirits back up.''

He wished he could make it so she never had bad days. He wished he could take her home and put her to bed and take care of things for her so that she could rest. It was odd to feel this way about her. He didn't remember ever wanting to protect anyone quite this way before. Without thinking, he reached out and cupped her cheek with the palm of his hand. She stared up at him, the question in her gaze, and he looked back and knew he still didn't have the answer.

Slowly she drew away, reaching out to catch Kevin as he ran past chasing the ball. "Come on, pumpkin," she murmured, pulling him up into her arms. "Let's go home. Mandy will be wondering where we are."

Grant walked them out to the parking lot and helped her settle Kevin in the car seat once again. He reached for her just before she slipped into the driver's seat. "Jolene," he said, then stopped, pulling back his hand.

She shivered. There was something in the way he said her name that sent a thrill through her, made her ache somewhere deep inside. "What is it?" she asked, searching his shadowed face, trying to see into the depths of his dark eyes.

He hesitated, not sure what he wanted to say to her. There was an emotion welling inside him and he didn't know what it was. "Nothing," he said quickly, suddenly afraid of it. "Nothing. Good night."

She nodded slowly. "Good night," she said softly.

He forced himself not to watch until her taillights disappeared down the street. But he couldn't go in, so he found himself pacing the dark, cold street, his mind racing. Tomorrow was the big day. He was finally going to bring Tony and Jolene together. There was no room for this crazy feeling that was nagging at him. He was going to do the right thing. He had to.

Ten

Jolene was back in the kitchen just a few hours later. All the cake layers were set out on the huge stainless-steel counter and she was ready to begin. Fou Fou had come in to help her and so had Grant. Very carefully, she placed the four foundation cakes on the cardboard she'd had the busboys cut and put the entire assemblage on the turntable. Working quickly, she frosted the top and sides of each with wedding cake frosting, then set the next layer upon them, first setting it on cardboard. Layer by layer, she built it up until the lightly frosted cake was basically in place, with a pedestal holding the top layer.

"We'll let it sit for an hour to let the foundation frosting harden," she told her helpers. "Then I'll put a thicker coating over the whole thing and get ready for the decorating."

They had coffee and sat around the table, telling stories and laughing softly. Each of them turned to look at the cake every few minutes. It stood like a model of a high-rise building just being built—its structure fine and full of promise. The first steps had been taken and they had been successful. They laughed a little louder, feeling just a little giddy, and luckily, Kevin was asleep in the break room.

"This is the fun part," Jolene noted as she began to mound decorator frosting on the areas where she would mount the roses she'd formed the day before. Working with calm deliberation, she formed a basis of green leaves to set them on, then brought the roses from the freezer and began to pull them off the waxed paper and place them, one by one, into a cascade that swept around the cake, from top to bottom.

"Oh, Miss Jolene," Fou Fou cried when she saw what was developing. "I never did see anything so pretty."

"Isn't it lovely?" Jolene agreed softly, her eyes shining. She couldn't help it. She was amazed at how well it had turned out. Amazed and very, very proud.

The wedding was at six in the evening and Tony was coming to pick the cake up at one in the afternoon. There was an excitement that was building as the others appeared for work and she wasn't really sure why. Everyone seemed to be walking on their toes, their eyes bright. Even Kevin felt it and was insisting on coming out of his playpen to be with everyone else. It was the cake, of course. It was gorgeous. She kept looking at it, wishing it didn't have to be eaten.

It should go in a museum somewhere. It's the most beautiful cake ever.

She laughed at herself for such fanciful thoughts but she couldn't help it. She was darn proud of what she'd done, and so was Grant. He was beaming and she basked in it.

"But wait," Picard said as two o'clock loomed near. He'd been playing hide-and-seek with Kevin and had just handed him off to Fou Fou to entertain for a few minutes. "Where's the couple for the top of the cake?"

Jolene sighed. She'd been putting off attaching the couple. The bride and groom had sent over the figures they wanted—comic instead of traditional—and she found them a little childish. Still, it was their cake, not hers. Dragging a stepladder over to the counter so that she could be in position to do it just right, she climbed up, steadied herself and prepared to put them where they belonged.

The accident happened too fast, and with so many things going on at once, it was difficult in later days to reconstruct how exactly it all went. Michelle had just opened the door to the kitchen and hissed, "Tony's here!" and Grant had turned to greet his brother, ready at long last to present him to Jolene, and Fou Fou was chasing Kevin to try to get him back into the playpen, and Jolene reached out to place the bride and groom on top of the cake. Kevin came running around the counter and crashed into the stepladder, Jolene let out a cry and began to totter. She tottered for what seemed like hours, hanging in midair with Grant watching her in horror. Everyone called out, "No!" and began toward her in slow motion. But nothing could stop the plunge. And seconds later, she had landed on the cake— just as Tony walked into the kitchen.

Grant seemed paralyzed, glued to his position. He looked at his brother, then he looked at Jolene who was rising from the cake with a face full of frosting. A violet rose dangled from her chin. A green leaf hung in her hair.

"Uh, Tony, I'd like you to meet Jolene Campbell," he said woodenly, but he didn't really expect to get a response. And then there wasn't anything else to say, and they all stood in stunned silence and gazed at the disaster that only moments before had been the most beautiful wedding cake in the world.

Tony was the first to break the spell. He turned, looking bewildered. "What...what just happened here?" he asked his brother.

"Uh, I think Jolene fell into the cake," Grant explained, feeling numb and looking it. He added quickly, "I don't think she meant to, though."

Tony shook his head slowly, beginning to awaken to the enormity of the entire debacle. He turned to Grant, wild-eyed. "What the hell am I going to do? I can't go back to the wedding with this."

Grant swallowed hard and looked at Jolene. She was staring at the cake and he figured she was too stunned to speak. She looked all right, though. At least she hadn't been hurt.

"We'll get you another cake," he told his brother reassuringly. "We'll buy cakes. Something." He cast about wildly in his mind but he knew he didn't have a solution. Not one that would work. But he pretended to. "Don't worry," he said hastily. "We'll...we'll have it there in three hours."

Tony looked incredulous, then hopeful. "You think so?" he asked, and when Grant nodded quickly, he added crisply, "Make it two." Turning on his heel, he left the room.

When the door slammed shut, everyone seemed to come back to life.

"Oh my God, look at the mess," Picard moaned, shaking his head.

"What are we going to do?" Michelle cried, wringing her hands compulsively.

"We'll have to just cart this thing away and..." Grant began, but a voice cut in and stopped his words in his throat.

"No!"

It was Jolene who'd spoken. She was standing before them all, her hands on her hips, her hair still caked with frosting, her silver eyes ablaze like those of a Valkyrie. "No one touches this cake but me," she commanded in a voice that would have turned sinners to stone in the old days.

Grant frowned, shaking his head. "What are you going to do?"

She gazed at them all defiantly. "I'm going to remake this cake."

They stared at her in shock. Finally Grant noted, "But...no one wants to eat cake someone has fallen into."

"I know that. Don't worry. They won't have to." She picked up a spatula and gazed at the sorry-looking mess as though she were planning the extension on a bridge. "I didn't fall into the whole thing. I know exactly what I'm going to do. You—" She pointed to Picard. "Get a plastic cutting board and hold it up here—" she indicated where "—so I can work against it. You—" She pointed at Michelle. "Get the extra layers out of the freezer. You—" This time it was Grant's turn. "Get Mandy on the phone and ask her to come take Kevin off my hands just this once. I need all my concentration for this job."

Everyone moved quickly, doing as they were told. Jolene worked like a surgeon, scraping away the unusable cake and preserving what she could of the rest. Meanwhile she had Fou Fou go to the storeroom and find big hunks of nontoxic foam, which she knew were kept there, while she worked at forming serving-size portions of cake from areas she couldn't save.

"We'll frost the extra layers and have ready cut pieces to bring out once they've done the traditional first cut," she told Grant. "We'll need paper plates and plastic wrap to cover each piece once they're ready to cut."

"That's a great idea," he told her. "But the cake...a third of it is gone. How are you going to...?"

"I know what I'm doing," she told him sternly. "Leave it to me." Turning, she ordered a cleanup from the busboys and told Fou Fou to mix up more batches of the frostings. Then she went to work on the foam, cutting pieces to take the place of the missing areas of cake.

"She's got the magic touch," Michelle whispered to Grant as she passed through the kitchen a little later.

He nodded. "I'm beginning to think there's a spell on me, too. But a bad one."

"What do you mean?"

He glanced at her, his exasperation with Fate showing through his usual good nature. "First I try to have Tony meet her casually in the kitchen and he mistakes Fou Fou for her. Then I plan to match them up at my mother's party and he takes off with you to go ghost hunting. Finally I arrange to have them meet under perfect circumstances, when she's just completed doing something for him and doing it so well, he was bound to be impressed. And what happens? She comes up for the introduction with frosting all over her face." He sighed wearily. "I don't think she made the impression I was hoping for."

Michelle laughed softly. "Ever think matchmaking might not be a major talent of yours?" she said, leaving him to think it over.

He turned back to watch Jolene. She was snapping out orders to the others and getting immediate cooperation. He had to admit, he was a bit envious.

"Whew," Picard whistled, winking at Grant. "If I don't watch out, she's going to take over my kitchen."

Grant grinned. "She already has."

He was skeptical at first, but she worked wonders with the frosting, spreading it over the foam until the areas of real cake couldn't be distinguished from the phony. And once roses and green leaves had been applied, the cake began to regain most of its former glory.

"Nice going," he told her as she finally turned from the work.

"I think I did it," she admitted, laughing softly as she looked up into his face. "I think I pulled it off."

He nodded, reaching out to take a chunk of frosting from her eyebrow and putting it in his mouth. "I know you did," he told her.

She wanted to kiss him but there were too many people standing around. He saw the impulse in her eyes and he winced, because it echoed his own instincts and he had to make sure it didn't happen.

"Look at this," he said to the rest of them, grabbing her hand and holding it up for all to see that it was as steady as a rock. "Nerves of steel."

"You'd better believe it," she said, eyes flashing as she turned to look at them all. "I'm just beginning to realize that I do my best work under pressure."

They opened champagne to celebrate and Jolene at first protested that she didn't drink, then drank greedily when given a chance. She really didn't indulge in alcohol very often, but this was a special occasion. And she was so very thirsty.

They loaded the cake into the van, along with the pieces they'd wrapped. "We can get it there by three-thirty," Grant said with satisfaction.

"But I can't go in like this," she protested, looking down at her stained clothes and feeling the stiffness in her hair where frosting still clung.

He hesitated. He would have liked to have made it as close to the deadline his brother had set as possible, but he relented. "We'll stop by my apartment. It's right on the way. And you can take a quick shower."

She agreed and they sped off. Jolene gazed at the sunlight with wonder. She had been so concentrated on the cake for the past few days, she'd forgotten real life was going on outside without her.

Grant's apartment was in a modern glass-and-redwood building on California Street with a sunken living room and piped-in stereo and carpets as thick as polar bear fur.

"Groovy," Jolene teased. "A real bachelor pad, huh?"

"It suits my purposes," he told her with a jaunty look meant to tease her right back.

She laughed and when he offered her another glass of wine, she accepted. She was feeling agreeably warm and lazy now, and the wine only added to the sense of well-being. She took a few sips and asked the way to the shower. "The only problem is, of course, that I don't have any fresh clothes to change into."

"No big deal," he responded easily. "Stephanie left a whole closet full of stuff behind and I've never cleaned it out." He pointed out her bedroom. "Take a look. You're taller, but there must be something that will fit you."

She walked slowly into the bedroom and pulled open the sliding closet doors. An array of fabric spread out before her, silks and rayons and combed cotton in all colors and designs. She reached out toward a blue dress, then withdrew again, just as Grant came in to join her.

No. She couldn't do this. She turned back and looked at him, shaking her head.

"I can't," she told him simply. "I just can't."

He frowned, puzzled by her reaction. "Why not? Half of them she never even wore. What's the problem?"

She turned away so that he couldn't see her eyes. If he didn't understand why she couldn't wear his ex-wife's clothes, he didn't understand a thing about her or how she felt about him. Didn't he know? Couldn't he tell yet?

"I just can't that's all. Maybe I could wear a shirt of yours, and maybe some old jeans or..."

He saw that she meant it and he didn't waste any more time trying to talk her into it. "Get in the shower and wash that hair," he told her, directing her through his huge bedroom to the bath that opened onto it. "I'll borrow a dress from my neighbor."

She whirled. "Oh, I don't know..."

"If you don't like it, you don't have to wear it. Believe me, the woman owes me. I take out her trash every week and I've sat for her dog. He's a schnauzer and a real menace. He dug up all my potted plants. Go take that shower."

She had to smile at him first. He was about the most adorable man she'd ever met. Then she scooted off to the shower, humming as she went, feeling deliciously wicked being naked in a man's shower. He'd set her wineglass on the counter and she finished it while she dried herself and slipped into a robe, and by that time the combination of the warm water and sparkling wine had her floating on air.

She heard Grant's voice outside the door and she opened it and emerged into the bedroom.

"What do you think of this?" he asked her, displaying a beautiful pale blue dress with slinky sleeves and a fitted waist.

"Ooh, I love it," she said dreamily. "Do you think it will fit?"

And then something strange happened. The robe began to slide off her shoulders. She could feel it beginning to happen, but somehow she couldn't seem to make herself care enough to stop it. *First the cake thing,* she thought rather irrationally as it slid slowly down her body. *Now this.*

"Jolene," Grant said, alarmed and reaching to catch the robe before it made its way to the floor. "Hey, wait a minute."

She looked up at him, smiling. "Why?" she asked him, her silver eyes shining like stars.

"Because," he said urgently, trying to get a handhold on the fabric that seemed to slip right out of his grasp.

But that wasn't enough of a reason for her, and she gave a little shrug and the robe took one final lurch and fell into a puddle around her bare feet.

"Oops," she said simply, staring up at him with huge eyes, eyes he could drown in if he didn't take care.

She was naked and as slick as a seal, as lovely as a picture, as fresh as the spring. His gaze took in her glowing skin, her high, swaying breasts with their tight, dark nipples, the curve of her hips, and he groaned with an emotion that came from deep down in his soul.

"Jolene, we can't..." he tried to say.

"Can't you?" She looked at him bravely and lifted her hand to touch his cheek. "I can."

There was no more resistance in him. Suddenly it was as if he would die if he didn't have her. She was like a flame and he had to risk it, he had to reach in through the fire and touch her. She filled his hands, filled his arms, clung to him, and then he filled his mouth with her taste and crushed her against his long, hard body and he became the flame himself, burning to make love with her.

She'd known for a long time that this was coming. Ever since that day at his mother's house when he'd kissed her, she'd known they were on a long road headed straight for this. He'd resisted and she wasn't sure why. She should be the one resisting, she knew that well. But she was in love with him, deeply, hopelessly in love, and she had to risk the danger. She had to wake him up to the truth that hovered between them, waiting only for them both to reach for it and make it real.

The air was cool against her naked skin but his flesh was hot beneath his shirt and she pressed closer, taking his heat for herself. His hands felt hard and strong as they held her, deliciously rough and caressing as they stroked her, and she closed her eyes and gloried in the sense of being loved.

He laid her down on his bed, spreading her damp hair out on the pillow, then tearing away his clothes. She let her gaze wander slowly down his body, gasping and beginning to writhe as he touched her. He murmured something sweet and dark in her ear and she smiled, pulling him down to join her, drawing him between her legs, capturing him with her thighs, lifting high and crying out with an ecstasy she could hardly believe when he came inside her. Such need, such demand, such pleasure—it was all so much more than she'd expected, the feeling so wild, so intense, that she clung to it, letting her body beg for more long after she should have been spent and satisfied.

His ragged breath coming in gasps, he rose above her and looked down, the wonder he felt shining in his eyes. ''Jolene, I never…''

He didn't finish the sentence but she knew exactly what he meant. She never, either. Never, ever had she felt like this. They were meant to be. There was no doubt about it.

Reaching up, she outlined the hard muscles of his chest with her finger, loving the feel of him, loving the way his back arched, the way his hips narrowed, the way his hair fell over his eyes as he stared down at her. But when she tried to see what he was thinking, she hit a stone wall.

''You're not angry, are you?'' she asked him, only half joking.

He shook his head slowly, then bent down to drop a kiss on her lips. The kiss was meant to show her…what? That he cared for her, despite the fact that he regretted what they'd done? It hardly mattered, because the kiss turned into two kisses, then three, four, and he lost count, because they were entwined again, rolling together across the bed and she was laughing softly, and he was amazed to find he was ready to love her again.

He knew he shouldn't. He knew it was despicable, what he was doing. But she was so soft and she tasted so sweet and when he stroked her nipples she made a tiny moaning sound that made him crazy and then he was inside her again and they were rising together, like the crest of a wave, and the sound coming from her was a growl of pure desire that turned everything white inside his head as they crashed in each other's arms, spiraling from urgency into ecstasy into total peace and joy.

"We've got to go," she reminded him as they caught their breath again. "We're going to miss the reception and we're the ones with the cake."

"What happened to romance?" he complained as he shrugged into his clothes. "What happened to sweet nothings in my ear?" He grabbed a jacket from the closet, looking at her quizzically. "It's just, 'Thanks a lot, Jack, now let's get going.'"

She turned, laughing, and let him kiss her one more time. Then she slipped the dress over her head and looked at herself in the mirror. She looked wonderful and she knew it. Her hair had dried in a mass of gold around her face and her cheeks were pink from lovemaking. The dress clung in all the right places and swished around her legs. She turned to see what he thought and his opinion was reflected in his eyes.

But not for long. Instead of saying what he thought, he turned away and started for the door. She followed, walking quickly to keep up with him, and he didn't say another word while they got into the van and drove to the church. And every inch of the way, her heart grew heavier.

What was it that bothered him? She couldn't figure it out. But every time she thought they had finally made a breakthrough, he retreated again. *This is not a good time to do that, Grant,* she thought to herself, biting her lip. *Not now. Not after making love to me as though you loved me just as much as I love you.* But looking at him now, you would never know he'd been such a passionate lover just a few moments before. She wished she knew what he was thinking.

Grant's mind was in turmoil and his thoughts weren't very pretty. He'd ruined everything, as far as he was concerned. He'd destroyed his own plans, finished off any hope of delivering this wonderful woman to his brother. He'd betrayed a trust, violated an oath, broken a promise—even though Tony didn't know he'd made one. But worst of all, he'd taken advantage of Jolene when he should have been the strong one. Just by making love with her, he knew he'd set up expectations on which he could never deliver. *What a jerk he was. What a worthless jerk.*

They found the church and backed the van up to the room where the reception was to be held. They recruited a couple of ushers to help carry in the cake, setting it on a long table. Jolene went to work right away, fixing a few little flaws, adding some fresh flowers to the arrangement of small pieces of sugared fruit around the base, setting out the slices of cake that had already been cut from the extra layers in the back room, ready to be brought out on a moment's notice.

And suddenly Tony was there, beaming.

"I can't believe it. How did you do this? This is magnificent. I've never seen a better cake."

"Jolene did it all," Grant told him, and Tony turned, smiling at her.

"So this is Jolene," he said, forgetting that he'd met her dressed in frosting just a few hours before. He took her hand and shook it warmly. "Thank you. Grant said you were a miracle worker and he was right."

She smiled back at him, looking into his eyes. They were similar to Grant's but not as dark and where Grant seemed to sink into your soul when he gazed at you, Tony seemed a bit distracted. He was very handsome, though, more polished than Grant, more mannered and reserved.

"I'm so glad you're pleased," she said softly.

Something in his eyes changed and she knew he was looking her over, liking the way she looked in the blue dress, regarding her suddenly as a woman and not just a pastry chef. But a small group of men came surging in to the room, calling out to Tony, and he turned to greet them and the moment was over.

She looked at Grant. He was looking at her oddly, searching her face as though he expected to find out something new about her at any moment.

"What is it?" she asked him, but he shook his head and didn't answer. The two of them walked slowly out to the van, got in, and drove off, leaving Tony, the cake and the wedding behind.

"You did a great job," he told her at last. "Thank you. I really appreciate all the extra effort you made to get things right."

She smiled and nodded. "And thank you for your help," she told him. "Couldn't have done it without you."

His old grin was almost back. "Sure you could have. You just wouldn't have had as much fun," he told her. They drove on for another moment in silence and when he asked the next question, she could tell he'd been planning it for some time. It was a little forced, a little too hearty. "Well," he said. "What did you think of Tony?"

"Tony?" She turned and looked at him blankly.

Grant nodded and glanced at her sideways. "Yeah. What did you think of him? Isn't he a great guy?"

There hadn't been much time or occasion to find out how great he was or wasn't. But Grant obviously wanted an answer. She hesitated, then answered very carefully. "He's your brother. I'm ready to think everyone you're related to is just fine."

"No, I mean really," he said, glancing over at her. "Don't you think he's good-looking?"

She smiled, admiring his profile. "Not as good-looking as you are."

"Come on, Jolene," he said, beginning to sound a little impatient. "You know what I mean."

She frowned, shaking her head. There was something downright odd about this conversation. "No, I don't really think I do."

He glanced at her with a look that said she was just being difficult. "Tony is an accountant you know. He's got a great little girl. Allison, she's eleven and…"

"Uh-huh." Hadn't she heard all this before?

Grant took a deep breath and plunged on. "Well, the one thing he needs is a wife."

"Oh. I'm sure he'll find someone eventually."

He was silent and suddenly a thought popped into her head. She remembered something from the first day she'd come to the restaurant, when he'd been giving her that crazy quiz and the most puzzling question had revolved around whether she could fall for a caring, compassionate and deeply loving, father of an eleven-year-old girl. At the time it hadn't meant a thing to her but now she realized he'd been talking about his brother, even then. Everything began to fall into place, all the bewildering talks about Tony, all the gentle coaxing and urging, everything that had mystified her all these weeks.

She turned on him, her eyes slowly widening. "Do you want me to go out with your brother?" she asked, hoping he would say she had it all wrong.

But he didn't do anything of the kind. "I...I think that would be great," he said gruffly. "If you two like each other." He swallowed hard, suddenly unable to go through with what he'd planned to say.

She sat still for another long moment, trying to digest this revelation. "I can't believe this," she muttered at last, looking out at the world passing by the window of the van. Everything out there still looked the same. Why did she feel as though she'd stepped into a looking glass?

Grant looked over at her and pulled to the side of the road, switching off the engine and turning so that he could speak directly to her. "Jolene, listen. My brother Tony is...I guess you can tell he's very important to me."

She nodded. "I'd say that's putting it mildly," she quipped.

"Let me try to explain it to you." He hesitated. This wasn't going to be easy. "See...our dad...well, he and I got along really well, and he and Tony were always fighting. Our dad wasn't a very subtle man. When he disagreed with you, he let you know it, and he always disagreed with Tony. Tony was always sure Dad hated him."

She nodded, not sure why he felt she had to know this. "Michelle told me some of this before."

"I know. But I want to try to make you understand. Tony did things for me..." He shook his head and started again. "Okay, here's an example. When I was sixteen, I started running with a bad crowd. Gang kids. I was acting up at home and being a regular louse to my family. Tony got wind of what I was up to and one night he showed up at the vacant house where we hung out. He told me he was taking me home. Tack—he was our leader—told him to get lost. He ended up fighting Tack to set me free from that place. I mean, here was this quiet, dignified guy fighting a big bully in order to save my soul. Can you see why I love the guy?''

Of course she could. And she loved him for loving his brother, for appreciating him, for his gratitude. ''Yes, Grant, I can see why you love him. What I can't see is why you would want me...'' Her voice trailed off. She could hardly put it in words.

But Grant wasn't through. ''The one thing I will always regret,'' he went on, ''was that I never told my father about what Tony had done. I was afraid I would get in trouble at the time, but even later...'' His haunted gaze met hers and he shook his head. ''Why didn't I tell him? I never let him know how brave Tony had been. He would have...I don't know. Maybe looked at Tony in a new way. But I never told him.'' He grimaced and added, mainly to himself, ''Why the hell didn't I tell him before he died?''

''He knew.'' She wasn't sure where the words had come from or why she'd said them. ''Grant, don't torture yourself about this. He loved Tony.''

Grant was staring at her. ''How do you know that?''

She shook her head. ''I just know it. When fathers treat sons like that it's because they want to coax the best out of them, not because they don't care. It's because they love them so much.''

She had no idea if she was anywhere near the mark. She only said things that came from her heart, and her heart wanted his pain to ease. Had she helped him at all? She didn't know. His eyes had a skeptical glint, but maybe there was a little hope in their depths. Maybe her words had gotten through to him.

Finally he spoke.

"So, did you say you would go out with Tony, or..."

Outrage swept through her, tearing away all compassion, all rational thought, and outrage like that had to find expression somewhere. "You scum," she began angrily. "You lowlife. You incredible jerk!"

"What?" His gaze showed absolutely no comprehension of why she should be angry.

Her eyes flashed fair warning of her own rage. "You've been setting me up for your brother all this time."

"Jolene, he's...well, he deserves someone like you."

"Someone like me?" She choked. "This isn't 'someone like me.' This *is* me. What do *I* deserve?"

He gazed at her earnestly. "Listen, Jolene, you couldn't do better than a guy like Tony."

She gasped, shaking her head. "You don't understand, do you? You don't have a clue."

"What?" he said again, looking completely blank.

She reached for the door handle. "I'm getting out right here. Let me go."

He grabbed her arm. "Jolene, wait, just listen."

She swung to confront him. "No, you listen. I quit. You got that? I will not stay anywhere near where you might be. I'm going to forget you and I'm going to forget I ever knew you. Goodbye."

She slipped out of the van and leaned in to give him one last speech. "And to answer your question, no, I won't go out with your brother. I don't want to have anything to do with anyone in your family ever again. Including you."

"Come on, Jolene. You don't mean that."

But she did mean it, and she turned on her heel and left him there.

Luckily, it was only blocks to her apartment, and she knew a shortcut that effectively lost him as he tried to follow her in the van. She ran up the stairs to her place, pulled the door open and flung herself inside, shutting the door and leaning on it, breathing hard.

"You were right, Grandma," she muttered, shaking her head. "Oh, you were so right."

And as she regained her equilibrium, she tried to teach herself to hate him. It was going to take a lot of practice, but she would do it. Somehow.

Eleven

The park was decorated for Christmas with garlands and wreaths. At a table near a fire pit, a small group was preparing a party. Jolene sat with Mandy on a park bench and watched people stringing balloons, at the same time keeping an eye on Kevin who was trying to make friends with a little redheaded girl.

"It's been six days now," Mandy was saying archly. "I've fielded all the calls. We've had Michelle asking if you would meet with her so she could explain Grant to you and we've had Picard panicking on the line because you won't come back and bake good things to complement his masterpieces and we've had Fou Fou just generally blubbering, for what reason wasn't quite clear, and best of all, we've had Grant disguising his voice and pretending to be your uncle from Dubuque. By the way, do you have an uncle in Dubuque?"

"Not that I know of."

"I thought not." Mandy laughed softly, shaking her head as she contemplated her friend's stern visage. "At any rate, haven't you punished them all enough? Not to mention the doldrums you've put me in. And I don't even know what it's all about." She raised an eyebrow. "That's a good place to start. Why don't you explain this little vendetta to me? What's going on?"

Jolene sighed as though the weight of the world were on her shoulders. "What's going on is the end of my life as I've known it," she said stoutly. "I have become a new person, Mandy. Tough, strong, sure, with nerves of steel." She winced, remembering where she got the latter description. "Nothing is going to shake me," she swore, ignoring the fact that something just had. "Or get to me anymore."

Kevin appeared before her, tears trembling in his huge eyes. "Mama," he cried, showing her his finger. There were teeth marks on it.

Jolene gasped. Outrage seemed just below the surface all the time lately. "Who bit you? That little redheaded girl?"

Kevin nodded, lower lip quivering.

Jolene rose with a snarl. "Where is she? Where did she go? I'm going to have a talk with that little…"

Mandy grabbed hold of her shirttail, pulling her back and laughing. "You'll do nothing of the kind, nerves of steel or not. Look at it. She didn't even break the skin."

Jolene glared at her friend. "Maybe not, but she certainly hurt his feelings." Still, she sank back onto the bench and pulled Kevin into her lap for comfort.

Mandy sighed, shaking her head. "Yes, I can certainly see the new woman in you," she murmured. "What a change."

Jolene kissed her baby's cheek and took a deep breath, closing her eyes. She had to calm down. This was getting ridiculous.

Mandy threw up her hands and smiled at them both. "Come on," she urged. "Let's get out of here. Let's go Christmas shopping."

Jolene sighed. "Nice try, Mandy. You seem to forget. I quit my job. We have no money."

Mandy shrugged, carefree as usual. "We can pretend, can't we?"

"I don't know." Jolene's brow furled as she thought that over. "Seeing what you want and not being able to have it tends to make one cranky." Her eyes took on a faraway look. "Very cranky," she repeated softly.

Mandy frowned. She knew Jolene was in love with Grant. Why on earth was she avoiding him? She supposed her friend would explain everything soon enough. In the meantime, Christmas shopping, even if it only involved looking in through windows, was the best she could think of as a distraction.

"Come on, you two," she said heartily. "Let's go walk through Old Town and look at the decorations at least. Want to go, Kevin?"

Kevin jumped off his mother's lap, his wounds forgotten. Eagerly he held out his hand for Mandy and looked back at his mother. "Two, nine, go!" he called to her, his latest way of saying, "Hey, let's go have some fun."

Jolene laughed. Kevin always brought her smile back. Rising, she joined the two of them and started off toward where the lights shone most brightly. That would have to do for now. And maybe for a long, long time.

It was only a few days later, however, when Jolene saw Grant again. Mandy was out with friends and she was alone with Kevin. When the doorbell rang, she assumed it was Mandy without her key and she flung the door open, only to find Grant gazing at her from across the threshold.

Her heart lurched and she put a hand on the doorjamb to keep from falling over. He looked so beautiful with his dark eyes and dark hair and smooth, tanned skin. She took in every bit of him in seconds, holding the sense of him to her and cherishing it. This was what she'd been missing. How could she have walked away from him? Her impulse was to reach for him, to hold him and never let him go again.

But first impressions could be deceiving. As she looked a little longer, she began to see that there was something wrong. He was swaying slightly, and his eyes didn't seem to focus very well.

"Grant?" she said questioningly.

He tried to straighten himself and failed miserably. "I have been drinking," he announced as though the neighbors ought to know as well.

A gurgle of laughter tried to surface but she refused to let it. "I can see that," she told him, glancing at the doors down the hallway and drawing him into the apartment before he could make another pronouncement. "How did you get here?"

He swayed again, looking around himself as though he were rather pleased with where he'd ended up. "Michelle drove me over." He looked earnestly into her face and tried to focus, blinking and widening his eyes. "She was very nice to me. She didn't want to see me get killed."

She'd never seen him like this before and she had to admit, he was rather appealing in a lost way. But she couldn't let him know she thought that. She looked at him with her hands on her hips, trying to be stern with him, but laughing inside. "At least you had the good sense not to drive in this condition."

His face took on a look of offended dignity. "I'm not stupid, you know."

She bit her lip to keep from smiling. "Well, that's still to be determined, isn't it?" she said with a significant look.

He frowned as though not sure what she meant and she took his arm and steered him toward the couch. "I think you'd better sit down," she told him, feeling maternal. "You're in no condition to stand, either."

He followed orders obligingly, but pulled her down to sit beside him, then turned to her and stared hard, as though he were trying to see down deep into her silver eyes. "I came for a special reason," he said haltingly.

"Really?" She tried to stare right back. "And what was that?"

He hesitated, then frowned. "I forget," he said sadly. Then his face lit up. "Oh, yeah. I remember now. I came to ask you to forgive me."

Her heart lurched again, but she managed to keep all emotion from her face. "Why?"

He looked puzzled by the question for a moment, then his face cleared. "'Cuz I want you to."

She shook her head, wanting to kiss him but not daring to do it. Not yet. "And you had to get drunk before you could come over here and do this?"

"Certainly," he said very seriously, enunciating every syllable with great care.

She stared hard at him, bemused. "Why?"

His expression quite obviously said that the reason should be self-evident to any rational person. "Because you're too scary to face without backup to my intestinal fortitude." He looked very pleased with himself when he managed to get the words out. "So I came to tell you, if you don't want to go out with Tony, it's okay."

She had to suppress the immediate reaction of irritation that came bubbling up with the name of his brother. It brought back all the reasons she'd been angry in the first place. "Well, thank you very much," she said, trying to hold back the sarcasm and succeeding only slightly.

But sarcasm was beyond his horizon tonight. He just didn't hear it at all. "No," he said sunnily. "I mean it. It's okay."

Her mouth twisted at the corners. "I mean it, too," she murmured, knowing full well there was no point in putting him in his place at the moment. He was bound to bounce right out of it again and never notice.

"You do?" That seemed to puzzle him but he shrugged it away. "I'll just have to find him another girl," he added casually. Just another task in the workaday world he lived in.

Her jaw dropped and she shook her head. "Oh, I see." She wanted to shake him. Was there no end to this devotion to Tony? "And where will this happy little search take place?"

He threw out an arm to show her. "All around. Everywhere. I'll have to search all the restaurants and bakeries in the Greater Los Angeles area."

"Restaurants and bakeries?" She couldn't think of a reason to do that and she made a face at him. "Why would you do that?"

His expression said, "Why, you silly," but even when inebriated, he was careful not to be mean. "I have to find him another pastry chef, of course," he explained patiently. "And that's going to be hard. Because—" he paused dramatically, then finished with a flourish "—most of them are men."

She coughed to cover her laugh. "So it would seem," she told him wisely, her eyes sparkling.

He nodded, glad to see she got it. "Men won't work," he told her earnestly. "Tony wants a girl."

Her grin surfaced. She just couldn't hold it back any

longer. The thought of Grant scouring the hinterlands searching for a pastry chef for his brother struck her as so sublimely ridiculous, throwing in the comment about Tony preferring women just seemed a part of it all. "Good for Tony," she said, and he nodded.

"Good for Tony," he repeated. Then he got another idea and jumped up from his seat. "Where's Kevin? I want to say hi to Kevin."

She rose quickly and stopped him. "Kevin's asleep."

He smiled at her, unconcerned. "Okay," he said, and started off toward the bedroom.

Grabbing his arm, she pulled him back around. "No, Grant. Don't go in there. You don't want him to see you this way."

"Why not? I'm perfectly fine."

He actually seemed to think so. She laughed softly, shaking her head, enjoying the feel of his solid flesh beneath the soft covering his sweater made. "No, you're not. You're perfectly soused."

He blinked. "That, too." Lurching slightly, he touched her hair, running it through his fingers and watching as it caught the lamplight. "Do you still hate me?" he asked her, looking sideways into her eyes.

She shook her head, her eyes misting. "I could never hate you," she admitted, her voice just above a whisper.

He closed his fist on her hair and let it slowly slip out between his fingers. "I missed you," he told her simply, and a lump rose in her throat.

Then he seemed to remember something and he frowned. "I mean, we all missed you, everybody at the Grill."

She didn't know what to answer to that, but it wasn't necessary to think of something, because he was swaying again, and a frown darkened his face.

"Hey, your room is spinning," he announced. Suddenly

his eyes seemed to glaze over. "I...I think I'd better lie down," he muttered, and she helped him back to the couch. He flopped out full-length and went to sleep before his arms and legs came to rest. She looked down at him, her love spilling over. His face looked young and sweet, his dark hair mussed adorably, and she wanted to throw her arms around him and hold him to her heart, taste his lips and feel his warm breath tickle her ear. For a moment, she felt she would burst with the feelings he brought up in her. Then a soft tapping at the door spun her around.

It was Michelle, looking just a bit sheepish, but stylishly dressed for it.

"Hi," she said, smiling as though she weren't sure of what her welcome would be. "I just came up to check on him."

Jolene smiled back and opened the door wide to let her in.

"He's out cold." She indicated where he lay on the couch.

Michelle took a look and bit her lip. "Oh dear. I was afraid of that." Turning, she gave Jolene an apologetic smile. "I'm really sorry, Jolene, but he insisted on coming to see you and I couldn't let him come alone."

Jolene reached out and gave her a quick hug. Her heart was full of affection for everyone tonight. Grant's visit had opened up a floodgate that had been closed for too long. "Come on into the kitchen," she told Michelle softly. "We can talk in there."

They chatted inconsequentially while Jolene puttered around the stove, making coffee and pouring it out for the both of them. But eventually the conversation had to come back to Grant—and Tony. It was inevitable.

"Grant tells me Tony was very impressed with the job

you did on that cake,'' Michelle said carefully at last, watching Jolene's eyes for her reaction.

Jolene shrugged. "What a day that was,'' she murmured. Then she looked sharply into Michelle's face. "You were in on it, too, weren't you?''

Michelle managed a look of pure innocence. "I don't know what you're talking about.''

Jolene groaned. "Yes, you do. You're a bit more subtle than Grant, but just as deadly.''

"Jolene…''

"Michelle, please understand." She opened her hands as though displaying a truth she didn't want the woman to miss. "I don't want Tony. I will never want Tony. I want…'' She took a deep breath and got brave, because she knew it was true and she knew she was going to have to face the consequences. "I want Grant.''

A deep look of satisfaction came over Michelle's beautiful face. "You're sure about this?''

Jolene nodded earnestly. "Of course I am. Can't you tell it's true?''

"For a moment there, I was afraid…'' Her voice trailed off and she closed her eyes, crossing her hands over her chest. "Thank God,'' she murmured like a prayer.

Jolene frowned, totally at sea. "What is it?'' she asked.

Michelle smiled at her, shaking her head. "Never mind.'' She leaned forward. "I have something I have to tell you.''

"What?''

"You're a very nice person, Jolene. You're a woman of the nineties, you're straightforward, you're open, you tell the truth. I'm from an older tradition. I get what I want by manipulation.''

Jolene shook her head, a frown between her brows. "I don't know what you're talking about.''

"Leave it to me.'' Michelle sat back and looked a little

smug. "I've got it all worked out. You'll go on the date with Tony."

"But..."

She grabbed Jolene's hand and held it tightly while she gazed steadily into her eyes. "You've got to. Grant's got it in his head that nothing else will do." Her smile was bittersweet. "It's a new twist. You've heard of sibling rivalry? Well, this is its opposite. We really need to coin a new word for it. Sibling guilt, maybe? Sibling regret? Whatever. In his mind, you're the best woman he's ever found, and he wants to present you to his brother, who he thinks he's wronged all these years."

"I know." Jolene shook her head. "It's so crazy."

"But it's Grant."

And she loved Grant. She didn't want to go out with Tony. But Michelle seemed to think this would work, somehow, and the way things were going wasn't.

"Once he sees you two weren't meant for each other, maybe he can relax," Michelle explained.

They talked for another hour before Grant woke up and groggily joined them, drinking one cup of coffee after another and trying not to meet anyone's eyes. But he couldn't resist looking at Jolene whenever he had a chance to do so without her knowing. What had he said to her earlier in the evening? He wasn't sure. He only hoped he hadn't revealed too much of how he felt.

Not that he was clear on his feelings. He only knew staying away from her had been the hardest thing he'd ever done in his life. Deeper than that would be too dangerous a place to go.

"Are you okay?" she asked him softly.

He looked up and got caught in her silver gaze. For a moment, he forgot what the question was. "Uh, yeah, sure.

I'm fine,'' he murmured, sitting up a little straighter. "Are you okay?"

Her smile was almost dreamy. "Yes, I think so."

And suddenly her hand was inside his and he held it tightly. *Like a friend,* he told himself fiercely. *Like a very good friend.*

Aloud he said, "So I guess you're ready to come back to work?"

She laughed. "Do you really need me? I heard Fou Fou was making the most wonderful desserts."

"Right. She burned the Baked Alaska and turned sponge cakes into hockey pucks before we managed to stop her."

Jolene simpered. "Well, if you really need me..."

"Believe me, we really need you. The steady customers are threatening to start a petition to get you back."

"Well, in that case, of course. I can't disappoint my many fans."

She was making a joke out of it, but he was serious. She was coming back. That made all the difference. His heart lightened for the first time in over a week.

Mandy came home and Michelle went out into the living room to talk to her while Jolene got Grant ready to head for home and his own bed. She zipped him into his jacket and smiled up at him.

"Michelle talked me into it," she told him. "I'm going to go out with Tony."

His face changed completely. "What?"

She searched his gaze. "That's what you want, isn't it?"

"Uh, yeah. That's right." Of course it was what he'd wanted. It was exactly what he'd been working toward for weeks. "That's great. I'll give him a call tonight and set up a date."

Something flickered in her eyes, but she smiled and

added, "Good. Michelle has been telling me what a wonderful man he is. I'm sure we'll get along just great."

"Yeah," he echoed, suddenly feeling queasy again. "Just great."

He followed her out to the living room and had a bantering conversation with Mandy, but all the time he was wondering why his heart was feeling heavy again. *Must be the aftereffects of too much alcohol,* he told himself. Sure. That had to be it.

Being back at work was wonderful. Everyone greeted her as though she'd been on vacation and they'd missed her. Kevin laughed and threw his arms around Fou Fou's neck, then danced through the restaurant, greeting every waitress, every busboy, as if they were long lost relatives. When he came to Grant, he stopped and stared for a moment. Grant grinned down at him, expecting to be called Cookie at any moment, but not caring a bit. Instead Kevin gave him a gap-toothed grin and said, loud and clear, "Hi, Grant."

Grant's jaw dropped. "What was that?" he asked, though he'd heard every syllable. Kevin didn't repeat it. Once was obviously enough. But Grant was thrilled and he swooped the boy up into his arms, racing back to the kitchen to tell everyone what had just happened.

"Honest, he said it very clearly," he insisted as the others gave him skeptical looks.

"Grant, Kevin can't really talk yet," Jolene said carefully.

"You should have heard him. Come on, Kevin. Say it," Grant urged.

Everyone looked at the boy and waited. He grinned happily, glad for all the attention, but not a sound came out of his mouth.

"Really, he said my name," Grant told them, beginning to feel a little frustrated by their lack of faith.

"Sure, Grant," Michelle said mockingly. "Let us know when he recites the Gettysburg Address along with it. Now that would really impress us."

While the others laughed, Jolene patted his arm. "At least he didn't call you Cookie," she whispered comfortingly.

He gave her a baleful look and retreated to his office, muttering to himself. Jolene looked at her son, wondering. But the rest of the day went by without him repeating himself, and soon they all forgot about it.

Jolene was so happy to be back, she spent the afternoon making éclairs for everyone before she got down to preparing dessert shells for the evening meal. It was wonderful to be with people she liked, even better to look up and find Grant looking at her from across the room, his eyes dark and dusky but somehow warm and provocative at the same time, reminding her of the time they spent at his apartment, of his arms around her and her body so responsive to his.

All right, she told herself. *I'll go out with your brother. I'll go out with him once. And that's it, mister. After that, if you don't want me, I'll...I'll...* That was where her plans hit a snag. What would she do? *Cry a lot,* she admitted silently.

She got Kevin home rather late that night, but Mandy hadn't yet returned from a hard day out looking for work. She'd been pounding the pavement lately, trying to get her dream of becoming a model off the ground. The modeling was supposed to be a stepping stone to getting back with Stan, and though Jolene wasn't sure that was such a good idea, she wished there was something she could do to help her friend. It was so sad to see Mandy come limping in with discouragement written large in everything from her face to her bearing.

She put Kevin to bed and put on a pot of tea, and Mandy came bursting in through the door right on cue. She flung down her packages, kicked off her shoes and threw herself down on the couch, but there seemed to be something odd about her tonight. Jolene frowned, noticing the difference right away.

"Well, you were right," she said, shaking her head sadly. "No one wants me to model petites. They laughed at me. Can you imagine?"

Jolene's heart sank and she came in and sat on the arm of the couch. "Oh, Mandy, I'm so sorry."

Mandy basked in her sympathy for a moment before she went on. "But all is not lost." She gave her friend a beatific smile. "I got a job."

Jolene's eyes widened. "Doing what?"

She held out her hands. "Hand modeling. I told you I'd done it before."

But Jolene hadn't known whether or not to believe her. "For ads?" she asked, not sure what this meant.

"Some ads. The agency I signed with does a lot of casting for television shows." She held one hand up to the light and studied it critically.

Jolene was completely at sea. "Television shows?"

"Sure. They always use hand models for the little movement scenes, like picking a lock or riffling through a drawer."

The light bulb flashed over Jolene's head. "You mean, that's not the real actress doing it when you see those scenes?"

Mandy laughed. "Oh my dear innocent. Of course not. The stars don't have time for such tedious work. They call in the hand models, and it pays very well."

"But...I don't understand." She shook her head, frowning. "How is this going to help you get back with Stan?"

"Stan?" Her eyes were wide and guileless. "Stan who?"

"Mandy!"

"Listen," she said, bounding up from the couch and beginning to pace the room. "This is going to be a whole new world for me. There may be a serious romance for me at the end of this road, but that's not why I'm taking it." She stopped and looked earnestly into Jolene's eyes. "I'm taking it because it's exciting and it's going to be fun. What will be will be. If I end up with someone I love, great. If I don't there will always be another road."

Jolene smiled and sat quietly as Mandy babbled on and on about her new job. There was one thing she was sure of: Mandy didn't love Stan. Jolene loved Grant, and that was how she knew. No job would have kept her away from the man she wanted. The only thing that held her back was the man himself. That, and the fact that Kevin was still her first concern.

She was going on this date with Tony and she had no idea what would happen after that. This was a step into the unknown. Maybe Grant would lose all interest in her once the date was over and it became clear that she was not going to fall for his brother, no matter what he did to make her. But she could hope for a different outcome. Hope, and maybe dream a little.

Twelve

The great date was set for the next afternoon. It was a Tuesday, the restaurant's slowest night, and Grant would take care of Kevin while they were out. He came over to the apartment while she got ready, pacing and muttering and scowling and generally acting as though this hadn't been his idea at all. She went serenely about the business of preparing for her date as though she cared. And when she came out and whirled in front of him, showing off her new cotton dress, she could see in his eyes that he thought she'd gone a little too far.

"You're beautiful," he said flatly, and she smiled.

"Thank you," she replied, gazing at him frankly. "I'm doing this all for you, you know."

His smile had a brave look to it despite the throbbing twitch at his temple. "And I appreciate it," he said woodenly.

Tony was at the door promptly, looking suave and prosperous. His eyes lit up when he saw her, and she began to glow under all this admiration. Grant noted the admiring looks that passed between them and suddenly felt uncomfortable in his light sweater.

"Is it hot in here?" he asked, running his index finger inside the neck to loosen it, but no one seemed to hear him. They were chatting, getting to know each other, and he seemed to be completely forgotten.

"Maybe I'll turn on the air conditioner," he suggested, though it was mid-December.

Still no reaction. They were engrossed in each other, it seemed. His frown deepened. "Or maybe I'll stuff my pants with ice cubes and go sit in the bathtub," he suggested, feeling a snarl coming on.

Jolene suddenly seemed to remember he was still there. "Ice cubes?" she asked, looking at him blankly. "I'm sure there are some in the freezer. If you want any drinks, there's a case of soda on top of the refrigerator."

"I don't think I'll need a whole case," he said, sarcasm dripping from his tongue. "I'm not trying to put out a fire."

But she didn't notice. Instead she was smiling sweetly at Tony. "Grant has offered to sit with my little boy tonight," she told him. "But I hate leaving him and I don't want to be too late."

Tony smiled right back. "You're a good mother, I can tell. Don't worry. I remember those days. My daughter, Allison, was always with at least one of us. Her mother and I wouldn't leave her alone with a sitter until she was three years old."

"You left her with Mama all the time," Grant protested, looking at his brother as though he hardly knew the man.

"Mama's not a sitter," Tony said, glancing over at Grant with an innocent look. "She's part of the family."

"That makes all the difference," Jolene agreed, nodding with him.

Grant looked from one to the other of them, wondering what had happened to his two favorite people. They were acting like cartoon characters, batting eyes at each other and everything. *Was this what happened when two people are instantly attracted to each other? What a revolting thought.*

"How's this?" Tony was suggesting for their evening game plan. "Dinner on the beach at a little seafood restaurant I know of. Then we'll walk around Balboa Island looking for Christmas lights. A lot of the yachts decorate really elaborately and then they sail around after dark so that their lights are reflected in the water. It can be a magical experience."

Delighted with his idea, she smiled at him. "Sounds wonderful," she told him, eyes shining. Walking quickly to the bedroom, she kissed her son goodbye, but he was too intrigued with the monster toy Tony had brought for him to pay much attention.

"Balboa Island." Grant moved uneasily, frowning at his brother. "Do you really want to go that far?" he asked.

Tony laughed at him. "It's only down the Santa Ana Freeway. We'll be home before midnight."

"Unless we're having too much fun to quit," Jolene added cheerfully as they went out the door.

Grant's scowl was fretful, but he wiped it away when she turned back to wave at him and she never saw it. He stayed and watched them leave from the window. He watched Tony escort Jolene to the car and then hold the door for her while she got in. He got into the driver's seat and started the engine and Grant could see that they were both laughing. Probably having a wonderful time. He swore softly, then stopped himself, shocked. Hey, wasn't that what he'd wanted?

The major ache starting up in his gut told him otherwise. He watched until their car disappeared from sight, hating every minute of it. He knew what he wanted to do. He wanted to go bang his head into a brick wall or two. But he couldn't do that. Not now. He had Kevin to think about.

He fixed the boy the meal his mother had left for him and played Hungry Hungry Hippos with him for half an hour, laughing with him at the silly little animals as they gobbled up their plastic chips, but all the while he was thinking about Mary and how Tony had loved her and how different Jolene was from his brother's first choice. Was she really Tony's type? Why had he thought she was?

Because she's your type, a little voice said deep in his soul.

"No way," he said aloud. She was nothing like Stephanie. Nothing at all. *But Stephanie was never really your type, the voice told him. And the way that relationship ended up proved it.*

The voice was right. When he thought about Stephanie now, he didn't even have a twinge of regret. Something seemed to have blotted all that out. The only woman who filled his mind these days was Jolene. He had to admit, he thought about her all the time. Hell, he was thinking about her right now, thinking about how those wild, exotic eyes of hers made his heart beat a little faster when he looked into their depths, thinking about Tony looking into those eyes. And, though he fought it, he was jealous.

"Hey," he said to Kevin, needing a change of scene to get his mind on other things. "Let's go over to my mother's house and play in her backyard. Okay?"

"'Kay," Kevin answered and raced to get his jacket.

Soon they were tooling down the avenue with Kevin

strapped into a car seat in the back and Grant teaching him songs he remembered from his own childhood. "A hundred bottles of beer on the wall..."

Kevin couldn't sing the words but he followed along, making appropriate noises and they arrived at Grant's mother's house in great spirits. She came out to greet them and walked around the house with Grant to the clearing in back, pointing out how well her Iceland poppies and pansies were doing, proud of her winter flowers. Together they stood and watched Kevin play on the equipment, chattering happily to himself and making absolutely no sense at all.

"So you finally came back to see me," Rosa said to her son. "And you brought the little boy with the beautiful eyes."

He looked at her, surprised. "So they're beautiful now, are they? I thought they were weird and menacing to you."

She shrugged, a faint smile lingering on her lips. "I'm getting used to them. Where is his mother?"

He took a deep breath and let it out again. "Out to dinner with Tony."

Shock registered on her face and then she turned away, starting back toward the house. He followed, trying to stop her, trying to make her see.

"Mama, why can't you understand this? I want the best for Tony. And believe me, Jolene is the very best."

She whirled and glared at him. "But you were kissing her."

He winced. "I know. That was a very bad mistake I made."

She shook her head and added softly, "Don't try to fool me, Grant. I saw it and I know that she was kissing you back."

He swallowed hard. This was very difficult to explain. "Yes, that is true," he admitted. "But that was before she met Tony. She's only just getting to know him now. Once she finds out what a great guy he is, I know she'll fall for him.''

His mother stared at him, searching his eyes. "And what about you?" she asked him softly. "You care for her, don't you?"

He didn't want to answer that one. "Mama, I..."

"Oh, Grant, Grant." She took his hand and held it between her own. "Don't you see the trouble you're asking for here? It's no good to make your brother happy by breaking your own heart."

His soul was twisted in knots. He only hoped the pain he felt didn't show in his eyes. "Mama, you know I won't ever get married again. I did such a rotten job of it, I've been inoculated. Marriage is not for me. But Tony needs a wife...."

"He does. But he can't take the woman you love."

He shook his head, his eyes tortured. He wanted to deny what she'd said, but the words wouldn't come to him. "Mama, they are the two best people I know, and they deserve each other."

"You're wrong, Grant. Tony deserves what he can get for himself. And this woman deserves a man who loves her."

He didn't have a chance to answer. Before he could get another word out, Kevin appeared on the pathway, walking bowlegged and carrying an Iceland poppy he'd pulled out of the ground, roots and all. Trailing dirt as he went, he came running toward Rosa and thrust it at her, his face alight with a cherubic smile. "Cookie?" he asked eagerly, handing her the flower in trade.

Grant stiffened, expecting fury from his mother. Her precious poppies were untouchable. But to his surprise, when he looked up, she was laughing.

"Look, Grant. He's picked me a flower."

"Uh, yes, I can see that."

"Oh, you little duck." She bent down to talk to the boy, beaming at him. "You can have a cookie. But don't pull up any more flowers. Okay?" She took the poppy plant in one hand and Kevin's little fist in the other.

Grant shook his head in wonder. If he lived forever, he would never understand women, that much was clear. She was leading Kevin into the kitchen and Grant followed gloomily, watching as his mother gave the boy two large round cookies, setting him up on a chair at the kitchen table to eat them. Then she turned to her bemused son.

"Oh, he's a natural charmer, just like you were at his age," she told him, patting his cheek with warm affection. "That's why it's always so hard to say no to you."

His frown didn't fade as he watched her move toward the sink and begin rinsing dishes. "Why does this sound like someone else to me?" he asked. He certainly didn't remember getting everything he wanted when he was young. "Maybe you're thinking of Tony."

"No." She shook her head and gazed out the window, through the flowers that sprawled from her window box. "Tony wasn't a charmer. Tony was too honest, too straightforward. If the facts weren't clear, he couldn't sleep at night." She laughed, remembering as she put a pot on edge to dry. "That was what used to drive your dad crazy."

Grant nodded slowly. "I remember."

Her face took on a thoughtful frown as she looked back and recalled things that she hadn't thought of in years. "He worried about Tony, you know. He wanted him to lighten up and take life a little less seriously." She smiled at him. "He wanted Tony to be more like you, for his own sake. He couldn't ever accept that Tony was the way he was and that he was happy being that way." She sighed, shaking her head. "He loved him so much."

"Tony?" Grant stared at her. "Dad loved Tony? You're kidding. I mean, he certainly didn't show it."

She glanced at him reproachfully. "Of course he did. You just didn't have the eyes to see it."

Grant made a face. "But did Tony?"

She dried her hands on her apron. "Oh, yes. Tony knew how much his father cared for him. Ask him if you don't believe me. I know what he'll say."

"But then, Mama..." He hesitated. He had never brought this up with her before, but he had been haunted by it for years. "Mama, why did Dad give *me* the restaurant?"

She looked at him, startled, then her eyes filled with regret. "You've felt guilty about that all this time? Oh, Grant, don't. Darling, didn't you know? He offered it to Tony first. Tony is the oldest, it was only right. But he knew all the time that Tony wouldn't take it. He didn't want it. He and Mary had their lives planned out and running a restaurant wasn't a part of the grand scheme they had together." She gestured with her hand. "You know very well Tony had no interest in it."

Grant stared at her, nonplussed. Of course he knew that. But that had never been the point. Their father's love had been the crux of the matter. If things were really as his mother claimed, why had he been so blind to it?

"But, Mama..."

"Tony and your father enjoyed sparring with each other. You're more like me. You don't care for confrontation with those you love and you do your best to avoid it. But Tony and your dad were alike in that way. I'm surprised you never realized that. They fought for the fun of it."

Her words were destroying a whole portion of what he'd

thought was his life and they were going to take time to mull over. He wasn't sure he bought it—the picture of the happy Fargo family didn't quite jibe with his own memories. Perhaps his mother was recalling life as she wanted it to be rather than as it had been. Whatever. It was still news to him that they had offered the restaurant to Tony, and that would take some getting used to. He needed time to think. He called Kevin and gathered him up for the trip home, starting off through the kitchen door, but his mother stopped him at the top of the driveway.

"You are coming for dinner on Christmas, aren't you?" she asked.

"Of course, Mama." He'd never gone anywhere else in over thirty years. "Where else would I go?"

"Here," she said firmly. "This is where you belong. And I want you both to come and bring whatever young women you are dating."

He looked at her, not quite sure what she meant by that. "No matter who it may be?"

"No matter. And I want that little boy..." She pointed to where Kevin was playing in the sand along the side of the driveway. "I want him here, too. I have a present in mind for him." She gave Grant a quick kiss and turned to go back into her kitchen. He stared after her for a moment, shaking his head. Sometimes his mother was a hard woman to figure out.

He and Kevin went back to the apartment. Mandy wasn't home yet and Kevin was getting sleepy, but Grant's mind was consumed with dark thoughts about Tony and Jolene and his father, all swirling around in his head, making no sense. He didn't notice how tired Kevin was until the boy crawled up into his lap as he sat on the couch, brooding.

He looked down, startled, but Kevin sank into his arms

as though he'd been there before and felt totally comfortable. Grant's arms closed around him automatically, holding him.

"Do you want to go to bed, Kev?" he asked him softly, enjoying the clean scent of his fine blond hair, feeling a keen sense of affection for the child that surprised him with its intensity.

Kevin leaned back against Grant's chest, his eyelids dropping, and murmured something unintelligible that ended with the word, "Daddy."

Grant's heart seemed to stop for a moment as he held his breath, wondering if he had just heard what he'd thought he'd heard. Had Kevin called him Daddy?

Kevin looked up sleepily and snuggled in more tightly. "Daddy," he murmured again.

Grant thought he would choke on the surge of emotion that came up from his chest. No child had ever seemed so precious to him before. "I love you, Kevin," he said softly.

Kevin nodded and his eyes closed.

Grant smiled, feeling a sensation of happiness he hardly recognized. This was new. This was really cool. All because a little boy had called him Daddy and he'd told that little boy that he loved him. Was this what life was supposed to be like?

But another question hit him in the pit of the stomach and he ached to know the answer. If he could say it to Kevin, why couldn't he say it to Jolene?

There it was, a new question to add to the others pulverizing his brain. He held Kevin in his arms, felt his heartbeat, listened to his breathing, while he slept. And all the while his jealousy was growing. He'd sent the woman he loved out on a date with his brother. What was he, some sort of crazy person?

There was no doubt in his mind that they could easily

fall in love. After all, he'd already designated them both as his favorite people. Why wouldn't they like each other just as much as he liked them? What he had probably done was set something in motion that he would regret for the rest of his life.

Kevin woke in half an hour or so, and it was a good thing he did, because Grant needed to get up and pace the floor. He did exactly that for another ten minutes, muttering to himself, calling himself names, while Kevin sat watching him, seemingly absorbed by his strange march.

"I've got to fix this somehow," he was muttering when Kevin slipped down off the couch to join him, aping his style and following right behind him. "I've got to stop things before they go too far." He stopped dead, struck by a thought. "What if he kisses her?" he asked himself. "What if...?" The thought was pure agony and he groaned, throwing his head back.

"All right. This is it," he said, his right hand balling into a fist, which he pounded into the palm of his other hand. Kevin was looking up at him and he copied him as best he could, making a fist and stamping his foot for good measure.

"Th's it," he repeated, his gaze locked on Grant's face. Grant stared down at him, gathering resolve. Finally he pointed at Kevin for emphasis.

"We're going to go and get her back," he vowed.

"We go," Kevin echoed, looking just as determined and wiggling his pudgy little finger in Grant's general direction.

Grant looked down at him and really saw him for the first time since he'd risen from the couch. He was copying everything Grant did, and once it got through to him what was going on, he began to grin.

"That's right," he told the boy. "You and me, Kevin. We'll get her back."

Kevin nodded stoutly and laughed when Grant swept him up into his arms. "Let's go," Grant said fiercely. "We're out of here."

The ride to Tony's house only took a few minutes. Grant parked across the street, unbelted Kevin and carried him up to the front walk. They were back. He could see Tony's car in the driveway. He turned toward the house and his heart sank. The lights inside were low, much lower than Tony usually kept them. What if he was too late?

The doorbell seemed to stick, and when he finally got it to work, it took forever for someone to come to the door. The door opened, and there was Tony, his shirt open at the neck, his hair slightly tousled, looking the soul of comfortable romance. Grant stood staring at him, unable to speak.

"Hey, Grant." His brother gave him a lopsided grin. "We were just talking about you. Come on in."

Grant entered cautiously. He saw Jolene sitting on a chair in the living room and he headed that way. Kevin caught sight of his mother and cried out, wriggling down out of Grant's arms to go to her. Jolene looked up, laughing, nearly bowled over as Kevin threw himself at her. Holding her darling close, she met Grant's gaze.

"Well, hello," she said. "What are you two doing here?"

There was a buzzing in Grant's ears and he had a sort of tunnel vision. All he could see was Jolene, and she seemed to be sitting in a shaft of light that lit her with a heavenly glow. *Like a Renaissance painting,* he thought with wonder. *Like a Da Vinci or a Botticelli.*

Aloud, he merely said, "We came to get you."

"To get me?" She looked surprised, even a little alarmed. "What do you mean?"

What did he mean? He still wasn't sure. He only knew he meant to take her away from Tony, keep her for himself. He shook his head, vaguely aware that his brother was standing a little distance behind him. "Tony, I'm sorry," he said evenly. "I can't go through with it. I can't let you have her."

He thought that Tony made some kind of choking sound but he couldn't be sure, because his attention was on Jolene. Her eyes had sparked with surprise at his words and he knew he was going to have to be firm or this would all end in disaster.

"Let's go," he told her, but her head went back and her mouth thinned and he knew it was going to take more than that. Glancing around, he was surprised to see Michelle was sitting on the couch. Where had she come from? Never mind, it was a lucky break, because he needed someone to take care of Kevin and Tony didn't know him well enough.

"Kevin, look who's here," he said quickly. "Michelle. I'll bet she wants to tell you a story."

Kevin looked up and chortled when he saw his old friend. Slippery as an eel, he escaped from his mother's lap and ran to Michelle, babbling in some strange language only he understood. "Will you watch him for an hour, Michelle?" he asked. "Jolene and I need to go have a talk."

"Of course," she murmured, but he didn't pay much attention. He had a grip on Jolene's hand and was pulling her to her feet.

"Grant," she protested. "What on earth do you think you're doing? You can't just grab me like this."

He knew she meant it but he also knew if he hesitated, he would lose. Instead of softening, he hardened, gripping her wrist more tightly and staring hard into her eyes.

"Come with me, Jolene," he said gruffly. "We've got to settle this thing once and for all."

She stared back at him. She had no idea what he really meant by "this thing" but she knew what she hoped he meant. In order to find out if she was right, she would have to go with him. Her heart began to race, because that was exactly what she wanted to do.

"Okay," she said at last, nodding.

And they went, striding quickly to his car. He helped her in and got behind the wheel, steering toward his own apartment. Neither of them said a word, but it was only a few blocks to his place and there was no need for talk.

She went up the stairs with him obligingly enough, but when they got inside his apartment, she turned on him.

"All right, mister. Do you want to explain just exactly what you are doing? You coax and cajole me for days to go out with your brother, and when I finally do, you seem to decide we're having too good a time, so you barge in and…"

He kissed her. It was the only way he could think of to make her stop talking. And she kissed him back, opening to him as though she'd opened her heart, leaving him breathless and filled with an urgency he'd never had before, a sense of desire that seemed to eat him alive.

He reached behind to tug down her zipper, still kissing her, and she laughed softly as her dress fell down around her feet. "What are you doing?" she cried, but she knew and she felt the need as much as he did. They pulled off clothing as though shedding barriers that had been between them too long, and when his arms came around her naked body, she arched into him, wanting to touch every inch of his flesh with her own, wanting him to crush her breasts against his muscular chest, wanting to melt into him and become one.

They came together right there on his thick silver carpet, crying out like hungry animals as the fire shot through them, driving them higher and higher, lighting up the darkness, reaching for eternity with all their will and all their strength, then laughing softly as they clung together on the slide back down to earth, embarrassed and delighted at the same time.

"It was just an excuse, wasn't it?" she whispered near his ear.

He nodded groggily, letting the warm joy seep through his body and into his brain. "That's right—just an excuse. I needed to make love with you one more time, so I decided to capture you and carry you away."

"I got carried away, all right," she admitted, smiling. "We're not supposed to be doing this."

"No," he said firmly, taking a deep breath and savoring how his body felt. "That was under the old rules. We're on the new ones now."

"Oh? And what do the new rules say?"

He kissed her neck and licked her earlobe. "The new rules say we're going to make love at least three times a day," he told her.

"Dream on," she said, laughing. Then she sobered. "But Tony…" she began.

"Can find his own woman," he finished for her, nuzzling her ear. "I found this one. Finders keepers."

Rising slowly, she looked him in the face, needing to know the truth. "Why?" she asked him softly.

"Why?" He stared up into her infinite eyes. He wanted to tell her why, but he couldn't. The words stuck in his throat. "What do you mean?" he said, although he knew perfectly well what she'd been after.

"Why have you changed your mind?"

He didn't answer. Instead he pulled her down into his

arms and buried his face in her golden hair and she lay against him, hardly daring to hope and yet, unable to keep from it. Was this a surrender on his part? Was he finally going to admit that he loved her?

Curling in beside him, she took another tack. "What did you want to talk about?" she asked.

He kissed her collarbone and let his tongue trace the outlines of her tight nipple, making her squirm and cry out softly. Looking down at her, reveling in the sensual response he could see in her eyes, he murmured, "I was lying. All I want to do with the rest of my life is make love to you."

And he proceeded to do just that, marveling at how she seemed to turn on at the touch of his hand, how she needed him as much as he needed her, how their bodies came together as though they were two halves of one whole, how quickly he could find the center of her passion and set it free—at how completely she satisfied him, and yet how quickly he needed her again. He'd never been this way with any other woman. This was special, and he knew he had to make sure he never lost her.

Still, it was hard to talk about it. As they rested in each other's arms once again, he finally turned and asked her, "What are you thinking?"

She responded with a smile, "I was thinking about something my grandmother used to say. 'When you get what you want, be quiet and enjoy it.'"

He touched her lips with his finger. "Is this what you want?" he asked her softly, and she nodded, closing her eyes.

That brought him uncomfortably close to the words he couldn't seem to say to her, so he changed to another subject.

"Listen, what was Michelle doing there in the middle of your date?" he asked her.

Jolene's head rose and she looked at him for a moment, biting her lip. Finally she decided to tell him. "She went with us."

He turned and stared at her. "What?"

She nodded. "Didn't you know that Michelle and Tony have been dating for the last two weeks?"

"Dating?" He looked at her blankly. "They can't date."

"Why not?"

"They're...they're..." His eyebrows rose as he realized the truth. "Oh, I guess they can, can't they? I'm so used to thinking of Michelle as a sort of sister."

"Maybe to you. Not to Tony." She smiled down at him. "She's been in love with him for years, you know."

He frowned, hardly believing his ears. Michelle? But he'd been around her forever. How could this happen without him realizing it? "How do you know all this?" he demanded.

"Women talk. And they listen. Men ought to try it sometime."

"Jolene..."

She stopped him with a finger to his lips. "And listen. There's more. I want to make sure you understand that I'm not interested in Tony."

He nodded.

"That I've never been interested in your brother."

"Okay, okay."

"That I only went out with him to teach you a lesson."

He grabbed her hand and kissed her palm. "I learned, believe me. I'll never mess around with matchmaking again."

She hesitated. That wasn't exactly what she'd meant. She wasn't sure she'd gotten through to him. Not completely.

But he was smiling at her and she relaxed, smiling back. What could she do? He was who he was, and she loved him that way.

They dressed slowly, teasing each other and remembering where and why they'd discarded each piece of clothing. They'd barely gotten themselves together before the doorbell rang.

Grant frowned. He didn't want this wonderful time with Jolene to end. "Who is it?" he asked at the door, his hand on the knob.

"Daddy!" Kevin's voice cut right through all barriers.

Jolene's jaw dropped, but Grant didn't notice. He was hurrying to open the door, and when he did, Kevin came flying into the room and threw his arms around Grant's legs.

"Daddy, Daddy, Daddy," he chanted.

Michelle and Tony came in behind him. "Sorry," Michelle said. "But he wanted to see his—" she was about to say mother, but something mischievous took hold of her tongue "—to see his family," she said instead, and Grant turned to look at her, hoisting Kevin up into his arms as he did so.

Family. She'd said family and he hadn't broken out into a cold sweat. There had to be a reason for that.

Sure there's a reason. Jolene's the right one. That's the reason, you idiot.

He swung around and faced Jolene. Kevin was still tightly clutched in his arms and he didn't feel like he would ever want to let him go.

"Jolene, I..." Once again words failed him.

"What, Grant?" she asked, looking anxiously into his eyes. "What is it?"

"Jolene..."

She reached out and touched his cheek with the palm of

her hand. "What is it, darling?" she whispered, her eyes full of sweet affection and joy. "Say it, Grant."

"I love you," he managed to croak out at last.

It was as though bells were clanging and horns were honking and general celebration had begun all around him, but then he realized it was only in his own head. "I love you," he said again, and this time it came out easily and he smiled instead of looking terrified.

"Grant my daddy," Kevin said, as though stating a fact that pleased him.

Jolene stared at them both. Tony and Michelle had faded into the background and she hardly remembered that they were there. But she knew Kevin was there. And she knew Grant was.

"I love you, too," she told him, loud and clear. "Forever. For sure."

And then they were all three together, hugging and kissing and laughing and not even noticing that Tony and Michelle had quietly left by the front door.

"My daddy," Kevin crowed again, and they both laughed.

"Are you sure you're ready for this?" Jolene asked Grant.

"Ready, willing and able," he told her, touching her hair.

And he knew it was true. This time, he was ready. It was going to be okay.

Okay, hell. It's going to be wonderful. It's going to be just right.

And looking down into Jolene's beautiful eyes, he knew he'd finally found out what his life was for. Together, they made something special. Together, they made a family.

* * * * *

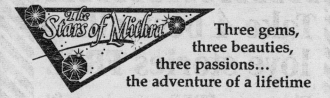

Take 4 bestselling love stories FREE

Plus get a FREE surprise gift!

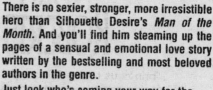

Return to the Towers!

In March
New York Times bestselling author

NORA ROBERTS

brings us to the Calhouns' fabulous
Maine coast mansion and reveals the
tragic secrets hidden there for generations.

For all his degrees, Professor Max Quartermain has a
lot to learn about love—and luscious Lilah Calhoun is
just the woman to teach him. Ex-cop Holt Bradford is
as prickly as a thornbush—until Suzanna Calhoun's
special touch makes love blossom in his heart.
And all of them are caught in the race to solve
the generations-old mystery of a priceless
lost necklace...and a timeless love.

Lilah and Suzanna
THE
Calhoun Women

**A special 2-in-1 edition containing
FOR THE LOVE OF LILAH and
SUZANNA'S SURRENDER**

Available at your favorite retail outlet.

SILHOUETTE WOMEN KNOW ROMANCE WHEN THEY SEE IT.

And they'll see it on **ROMANCE CLASSICS**, the new 24-hour TV channel devoted to romantic movies and original programs like the special **Romantically Speaking—Harlequin™ Goes Prime Time.**

Romantically Speaking—Harlequin™ Goes Prime Time introduces you to many of your favorite romance authors in a program developed exclusively for Harlequin® and Silhouette® readers.

Watch for **Romantically Speaking—Harlequin™ Goes Prime Time** beginning in the summer of 1997.

If you're not receiving ROMANCE CLASSICS, call your local cable operator or satellite provider and ask for it today!

Escape to the network of your dreams.

See Ingrid Bergman and Gregory Peck in *Spellbound* on Romance Classics.

As seen on TV!
Free Gift Offer

With a Free Gift proof-of-purchase from any Silhouette® book,
you can receive a beautiful cubic zirconia pendant.

This gorgeous marquise-shaped stone is a genuine cubic
zirconia—accented by an 18" gold tone necklace.

(Approximate retail value $19.95)

Send for yours today…
compliments of *Silhouette*®

To receive your free gift, a cubic zirconia pendant, send us one original proof-of-purchase, photocopies not accepted, from the back of any Silhouette Romance™, Silhouette Desire®, Silhouette Special Edition®, Silhouette Intimate Moments® or Silhouette Yours Truly™ title available at your favorite retail outlet, together with the Free Gift Certificate, plus a check or money order for $1.65 U.S./$2.15 CAN. (do not send cash) to cover postage and handling, payable to Silhouette Free Gift Offer. We will send you the specified gift. Allow 6 to 8 weeks for delivery. Offer good until March 31, 1998, or while quantities last. Offer valid in the U.S. and Canada only.

Free Gift Certificate

Name: _____

Address: _____

City: _____ State/Province: _____ Zip/Postal Code: _____

Mail this certificate, one proof-of-purchase and a check or money order for postage and handling to: SILHOUETTE FREE GIFT OFFER 1998. In the U.S.: 3010 Walden Avenue, P.O. Box 9077, Buffalo, NY 14269-9077. In Canada: P.O. Box 613, Fort Erie, Ontario L2Z 5X3.

FREE GIFT OFFER   084-KFD
ONE PROOF-OF-PURCHASE
To collect your fabulous FREE GIFT, a cubic zirconia pendant, you must include this
original proof-of-purchase for each gift with the properly completed Free Gift Certificate.

084-KFDR2

SUSAN MALLERY

**Continues the twelve-book
series—36 HOURS—in
January 1998 with
Book Seven**

THE RANCHER AND THE RUNAWAY BRIDE

When Randi Howell fled the altar, she'd been running for her life! And she'd kept on running—straight into the arms of rugged rancher Brady Jones. She knew he had his suspicions, but how could she tell him the truth about her identity? Then again, if she ever wanted to approach the altar in earnest, how could she not?

For Brady and Randi and *all* the residents of Grand Springs, Colorado, the storm-induced blackout was just the beginning of 36 Hours that changed *everything!* You won't want to miss a single book.

Available at your favorite retail outlet.

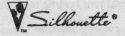